She struggled with the leve
changed my mind. Okay? N

"Beth, stop it! If you keep
going to catch up with you aga   ....
face it, you gain that power back."

She let go of the lever and sat still. She slowed her breathing down and gripped the steering wheel tightly. She looked into the rearview mirror directly at the headlights. They suddenly went dark. I turned around to see the vehicle. There was a haze around it, so it was still difficult to see. Beth opened the car door with no problem. She glared at me with a disdain in her eyes I hadn't seen before.

"You're a persistent son of a bitch," she said. "Aren't you?"

"I'm only trying to help you," I said.

"Well, come on then. Let's end this mystery together."

She got out of the car and closed the door. I climbed out of the passenger's side and came around behind her. In the mist, the other vehicle's door opened, and the sound of footsteps hit the pavement. A shadowy figure closed the door and walked toward us. As it approached, a scraping sound emanated from the concrete, growing louder as it got closer. When the figure finally emerged, standing before Beth as clear as day and holding a shovel in one hand, I froze.

WHEN BETH WAKES UP

by Matthew Franks

Chapter One

Someone tried to murder Beth Martin. Seeing her lie peace-fully on her hospital bed, attached to a breathing machine and an IV providing vital fluids, one might think she was just sleeping. But, unfortunately, she wouldn't be waking up any-time soon. As a result, getting information about who tried to kill her proved to be a bit of a challenge. But then, if it had been easy, they wouldn't have called me.

I sat beside her in a plastic chair, contemplating my next move. I had never entered the mind of someone in a coma before, so I really didn't know what to expect. There was a good chance I would go in only to bounce right back out, sort of like the way the tide pushes you back to shore when it gets too high. Or I could go in and find nothing, a blank slate that offered no answers. Whatever the case, I wasn't going to do her any good sitting there and staring at her.

I took a deep breath and focused on her face. Her light brown hair was pulled back out of the way so I could project without hindrance. A long, cylindrical spiral of light emitted from my forehead and attached to hers. I felt all my psychic energy flow toward her and, within seconds, was inside her mind.

It was cloudy at first. It was as if I were walking through a fog only to see it lift and disappear completely. After the haze cleared, I found myself in the center of a golf course.

Beautiful, rolling hills spread out in all directions. I could see a building in the distance. People were sitting at elegantly clothed tables on a veranda having lunch. I started walk-ing toward the building when a golf cart zoomed past, nearly knocking me down.

"Hey!" the driver called to me as he barreled along. "Get off the green, buddy!"

I heeded his words and moved more quickly in the direction of the building. When I reached the veranda, I saw her. Sitting at a table by herself and sipping a cocktail was Beth Martin. Only she wasn't in a hospital gown hanging on for her life. She was dressed in a long, flowing white dress. Her hair fell past her shoulders, cascading down her arms. I started toward her when a waiter blocked my path.

"Excuse me, sir," he said. He was an older man in his early sixties. "Do you have a reservation?"

I hesitated. "Yes," I finally answered. "As a matter of fact, I do. The name's Max Crawford. I made the reservation last Friday."

He held up a small pad and looked through a list of names. "I'm sorry," he said, shaking his head. "But you're not on the list."

"Could you maybe check with your manager?" I said, wishing he would just go away. "I'm sure it's just an oversight."

"Fine," he scoffed. "But if you don't have a reservation, you'll have to leave immediately."

"Of course," I agreed.

He wandered off toward the building. I waited until he was out of sight and walked among the tables to get to Beth. I noticed the people sitting at the tables were all very different from each other. At one table, a teenage girl was cuddled up with a boy wearing a Ramones t-shirt and sporting a faux hawk. At another table, three high-society women were in a circle scarfing down their lunches as if their lives depended on it. At another table, a middle-aged man in a postman's uniform was showing his five-year-old daughter a magic trick.

When I made it to Beth's table, she looked up at me curiously. "Can I help you?" she asked.

"Actually, I was hoping I could help you," I said. "Do you mind if I sit?"

"Not at all," she said, motioning to the empty chair across from her.

"Thank you," I said and sat down. "So…have you been a

member of this country club very long?" I asked.

"It isn't a country club," she said. "Who did you say you were again?"

"I didn't actually," I said. "My name's Max." I extended my hand. "Max Crawford."

She hesitantly took my hand and shook it. "Margaret," she said. "Margaret Stevens."

"Margaret Stevens?" I said, a little taken aback. "Do you go by any other name?"

"That's the one I was given," she said, letting go of my hand.

"Listen, Mr. Crawford, I'm not sure what this is about but—"

"Sorry. I'll get right to the point." I leaned in toward her. "I was sent here by the FBI. You were…a woman named Beth Martin was hurt by someone very badly. They want me to find out who did it."

She shrugged. "I don't know anyone named Beth Martin. I'm afraid I can't help you."

The waiter from earlier returned. "Sir," he said to me. "It appears that you do not have a reservation and, as such, will be required to leave immediately."

I looked at Beth, who looked back at me with an almost vacant stare, and then at the waiter. It was obviously going to be a lot harder than I hoped. Realizing I was going to need to be very careful how I approached Beth, or whatever she called herself, I stood up and pushed my chair in under the table.

"Sorry to bother you," I told her. "Enjoy your lunch."

"Wait a minute," she said. "This woman you told me about. Is she going to die?"

"I don't know."

"Well, I'll hope for the best."

"I'm sure she'd appreciate that." I paused for a moment to gauge her reaction. When she didn't bat an eye, I knew I had my work cut out for me. "Good day, Ms. Stevens."

"Good day, Mr. Crawford."

I left her and walked past the waiter toward the back entrance of the restaurant. I opened the door as if to leave through the front only to unexpectedly enter a high school classroom. A teacher stood before a full class of students and pointed to some numbers written on a chalkboard. They were random. "2-6-7-21-31." She was standing quietly as if anticipating one of them to speak.

"No one wants to try to solve the problem?" she said, looking around the room. She noticed me standing in the back of the room. "I'm sorry. Can I help you?"

"Oh, no," I said. "I'm just observing."

"And who are you?"

"I'm a…district representative."

"Very well," she said then turned back to the class. "Okay. If no one wants to volunteer, I'll just pick someone." She looked toward the front of the class and her eyes stopped on the same teenage girl that was cuddled up to the young man in the Ramones t-shirt at the restaurant. "Miss Martin, why don't you come up and try to solve the problem?" she said to her.

The young woman stood up and looked around at her peers. They all stared at her blank faced. Even her boyfriend had a vacant look. She moved to the front of the room and scanned the numbers on the board. The teacher held out a piece of chalk and the young woman took it hesitantly. She pressed the chalk to the board and started writing a number, but her hand began to shake. Pretty soon her whole body was trembling, and she dropped the chalk to the floor.

She turned to the class and opened her mouth to speak but couldn't. She grunted a few times like she was in pain and then held her hands to her face. She dug her fingernails into the skin on either side of her nose and started pulling it off, exposing slimy, red flesh underneath.

Some of the class screamed as they watched in horror. Others ran to the door to escape but the door was locked. She continued to pull her face off, revealing a crimson creature with huge, black eyes and a salivating, sharp-toothed mouth.

"Now you listen here, Miss Martin," the teacher said to her as if she had merely stolen cookies from the jar. "Enough of this nonsense or I will call your parents immediately!"

The creature let out a piercing yelp and ripped off the rest of the human body as if it were shedding clothes. The teacher pulled a fire extinguisher off the wall and sprayed the creature with it. The creature fell to the ground and squealed like a wounded animal and then disappeared completely. And then the class and the teacher were gone too. All that remained were the numbers on the chalkboard.

I walked over to the board and memorized the numbers. They might've meant nothing, but I was desperate for clues. I turned to leave and noticed a charcoal-colored outline of where the creature had fallen on the floor. I leaned down and ran my finger over the substance. It felt warm and smelled like tar. Deciding it was time to move on, I walked to the door and discovered that it was conveniently unlocked.

I stepped out of the classroom and into a lobby area that had several plush chairs and expensive couches arranged around a man playing soft classical music on a piano. There was a fountain nearby and a row of men and women wearing tan pants and white shirts behind a counter at the forefront of the room. I casually strolled over to the counter and stopped at the first one. She was a red-headed, freckled young woman who couldn't have been a day over twenty-one.

"May I help you, sir?" she asked with a smile that revealed braces on her teeth.

"I hope so," I answered. "What is this place?"

She giggled. "What do you mean?"

"Is it a country club? A high school? A five-star hotel? Or all of the above?"

"I'm afraid I can't help you, sir."

"Why not?"

"Because I don't know what it is," she said, abruptly turning pale as if she'd just seen a ghost. "I just work here."

Before I could ask another question, the waiter from outside came over from nowhere and cleared his throat. I didn't look at him, hoping he would go away. He cleared it again, only louder this time. The red-headed girl began to hyperventilate. The waiter stepped between us and scowled at me.

"I asked you nicely to leave, sir," he said. "And now you're upsetting a member of our staff. Do I need to call security to escort you out?"

"I don't know. Would they have any answers?"

The waiter leaned over the counter and pressed a red button. A loud siren went off above our heads. The girl and all the other people behind the counter suddenly ducked down out of sight. I turned to see two strange beings coming toward me. Wearing the same tan pants as the counter staff, their bottom half appeared human. Their top half, on the other hand, was much more alien. Dozens of glowing, yellow tentacles stemmed from torsos—the same charcoal color that was on the floor of the high school classroom. Their green, oval-shaped heads were too big for their bodies, making their dark, beady eyes and tiny mouths grossly disproportionate to their faces. They stopped at the counter and gave me a once-over.

"Is this man causing trouble?" one of them lisped through thin, avocado lips.

"As a matter of fact, he is," the waiter answered the creature. "He needs to be removed."

The two "security guards" reached out their tentacles and wrapped them around me. They felt like wet noodles tying my arms to my sides. I could've easily broken free, but I didn't want to be a threat to Beth's psyche. Instead I stood still and let the creatures lead me away from the counter and to the front entrance. They escorted me outside into the open air and released their flimsy grip on me.

"Don't come here again!" one of them hissed.

They went inside and slammed the door in my face. I took several steps back to get a better perspective and noticed that the front of the building looked more like a nursing home than a hotel. There were half a dozen empty rocking chairs in a row under an awning and neatly trimmed shrubs lined uniformly along a sidewalk leading to the porch. It was a definite contrast to the rest of my disjointed experience.

Still scratching my head as to how everything connected, I decided I would have to come up with a better strategy for when I returned. Right as I was about to withdraw from Beth's mind, I saw a waist high marquee sign on the ground to my left. It said, "Saint Stephen's Home For The Recently Emancipated." Underneath was a second line in a smaller font that read "Where Fancy Doth Not Make Clean."

Chapter Two

The day before, I was sitting in Warden Pinkerton's office at the State Penitentiary in Huntsville, Texas. Every quarter, I would meet with him to discuss the rehabilitation work I did with inmates. For fourteen years, I entered prisoners' dreams to try to help them see the error of their ways and, for fourteen years, the warden would sign off for me to continue. But that was all coming to an end.

"They're shutting down the program, Max," he said behind his oversized mahogany desk.

He was a short, robust bald man who was always sweating even when it was freezing.

Sometimes, during our meetings, I would watch beads race down his forehead and wonder which one would reach his cheeks first. Even more of a distraction, when he leaned back in his chair, the huge bear head mounted on the wall behind him looked like it was perched on top of his perspiring scalp.

"They can't do that!" I protested. "Don't they realize how much has been accomplished?"

"Yes, but it's not enough," he said. "You've helped a lot but what about the ones that leave here and commit another crime? I hardly call that rehabilitated."

"Whose side are you on, Jim?"

"I'm on your side, Max. You know I've supported you from the very beginning. The feds had to make lots of cuts. You just happened to be one of them. I'm sorry."

"I understand," I said and stood.

He got up from behind his desk and extended his hand. "It's been a pleasure."

I looked at him for a second to read his thoughts. The truth was he couldn't have cared less about me or the program. He was a puppet of the system and did what he was told. I accepted his handshake despite his sweaty palm squishing up against mine. That was one thing I wouldn't miss.

"Listen," he continued, letting go of my hand. "If you need a reference or anything, let me know."

"Thanks, Jim. How long do I have?"

"A week," he answered. "Feel free to take that time to get everything squared away."

Intensive dream therapy with dangerous, convicted criminals isn't something you simply "square away" but there was no use telling him that. Still, a week was better than nothing. With the time I had left, I would increase sessions with the ones more susceptible to change and hope for the best. I wanted to be angrier about the whole thing but couldn't. Fourteen years was a good run for something so unconventional.

I went back to my office on the other side of the prison and sat down at my desk. I picked up a picture of my wife, Jessica, and my daughter, Katie. Jessica had been a kindergarten teacher for six years and Katie was in the eighth grade. I couldn't believe how quickly time had gone. I set the picture down and grabbed my cell phone off the desk. I was about to call Jessica when the phone buzzed in my hand and her picture popped up on the screen.

"Hey," I answered. "I was just about to call. I wanted to tell you—"

"Are you busy?" she interrupted.

"Not particularly. Why?"

"It's Katie," she said. "There was an incident at school. Her principal wants to see the three of us this afternoon."

"What happened?"

She sighed. "Apparently she heard another student call her a 'bitch' and shoved her into a locker. A teacher broke it up before it got bad."

"Did the student call her a 'bitch'?"

"I don't know. There were several students around that didn't hear her say it. According to them, Katie walked up out of nowhere and pushed her."

"That doesn't sound like Katie. The other students are probably ganging up against her."

"Or..." she paused for a moment. "It could be that the student just thought it and didn't actually say it out loud."

"But how is that possible? She—"

I stopped and nearly dropped the phone. There are many "firsts" in a child's life that a parent never forgets. Her first word. The first time she walks. Even the first time she slams her door in your face because she doesn't get to go to a friend's house even though the whole school is going. One "first" that most normal parents never experience, however, is when she reads someone's mind for the first time because her psychic father passed on the ability to her.

"I'm sure there's another explanation," I said, trying to deny it.

"Let's hope so," she said. "Can you be at the school at three thirty?"

"Yeah," I said, quietly wishing that the other students were just jerks.

"Good. Barbara's covering my afternoon duty, so I can go. What were you trying to say earlier?"

"It can wait," I told her. "Let's get Katie sorted out first."

I left a short while later and was in my car on the way to Frederickson Junior High. I'd been there many times to pick Katie up after school. Before that, I used to pick her up at her elementary school and she'd go on and on about her day, barely leaving me a second to get a word in edgewise. Now, she'd just sit in the back seat with a singular vocabulary. "Did you have a good day?"

"No."

"Did something bad happen?"

"No."

"Do you know any words other than 'no'?"

"No."

When I arrived at the school, Jessica was already in the parking lot. As soon as I pulled up next to her car, she got out and gave me a little frown through the passenger window. She always made that face when there was something potentially wrong. Every time I saw it, I'd have given anything to see it curl up into a smile. I put the car in park and got out to meet her.

We went inside together and checked in at the front office. The secretary had us sit down and wait. It reminded me of times I went to the principal's office as a kid and had to wait. That was always the worst part. Once you got in, he gave you a scolding or called your parents then it was over. It was the anticipation that drove you mad as the loudest wall clock in the world slowly ticked the minutes away above your head.

It wasn't long, however, before Katie came into the office and plopped down in the seat across from us. She was wearing her gym clothes, a t-shirt with Frederick Junior High on it and a pair of shorts that in my opinion needed a couple more inches. She slammed her books on the floor and crossed her arms without acknowledging us.

"Good to see you too, peanut," I said.

"This is so stupid," she said, rolling her eyes. "She didn't even get hurt."

"Well, she could have," Jessica piped in. "You can't just go around pushing people."

"Yeah, well, you can't go around calling people a 'bitch' either."

"Keep your voice down," Jessica told her. "Your father and I are very disappointed." She nudged me. "Right?"

"Yes," I said. "Very disappointed. You can't let people push your buttons. It's—"

Before I could finish, the principal, Mr. Gladwell, stepped out of his office and cleared his throat. "Mr. and Mrs. Crawford," he said. "You may come in now."

We all stood up and followed him in. His office was a standard size with framed college diplomas on the wall next to a signed picture of him with a hockey player. There were three little chairs across from his plush desk chair. He motioned for us to sit and closed the door behind him. Jessica and I sat but Katie stayed standing.

"Sit down, young lady," Jessica told her.

"Fine," she said and took the seat on the end.

Mr. Gladwell sat at his desk and leaned forward. "Thank

you for agreeing to see me today," he said. "I wish it were under better circumstances."

"Well, we can assure you it won't happen again," Jessica began.

"I'm glad to hear that. Normally this sort of thing requires the student to be suspended but if Katie were willing to apologize—"

"I'm not apologizing to her!" Katie cut him off. "If anything, she needs to apologize to me!"

"Katie, that's enough!" Jessica told her. "I'm sorry, Mr. Gladwell. She's not normally like this."

He held his hand up. "No need to apologize," he said. "Kids at this age can be tenacious." He glanced at me then back at Jessica. "I'm sure you're doing the best you can," he added, holding his gaze on Jessica a moment longer.

"Gross!" Katie blurted out.

"What is wrong with you?!" Jessica asked her.

"It's not me!" She pointed to Mr. Gladwell. "It's him! He just said he wants to see you naked! You didn't hear that?!"

Mr. Gladwell blushed. "I said no such thing!"

"Yes, you did!" Katie shouted. "You didn't hear that?!" she asked Jessica.

"No," Jessica replied, turning toward me with the same half-frown from earlier.

"Dad?!" Katie said pleadingly.

I checked Mr. Gladwell's thoughts to confirm and he was, in fact, frantically attempting to erase images of Jessica unbuttoning her blouse from his mind and replace them with images of an older woman who I assumed to be his grandmother. I sighed. I really didn't want this for Katie. There were already enough issues to overcome during adolescence. Thinking that you're hearing voices shouldn't be one of them.

"Mr. Gladwell," I said, leaning forward in my chair. "It seems to me that my daughter is going through quite a bit of stress. Junior high can do that to you. I'm sure you understand."

He cleared his throat. "Of course," he said, trying to maintain professionalism.

"I wonder if you wouldn't consider allowing my wife and

me to address the matter ourselves at home. We assure you that it won't happen again."

I wanted to add "you horny bastard" but that would've blown his mind even more and, frankly, he was already looking discombobulated. He paused for a moment, allowing more time for the images of the older woman to dominate his thoughts. And then they disappeared completely, leaving a relatively blank slate in his mind that made him only slightly less embarrassed.

"That will be fine," he said, no longer making eye contact with any of us. "Now if you'll excuse me, there's a meeting I have to attend."

Katie hopped out of her seat and was out the door. Jessica and I went after her, finally catching up with her in the front of the school. She was sitting on a bench near the parking lot, wiping tears away. It reminded me of the time we were at the park and she fell and hurt her knee. I sat next to her and put my arm around her, but she pushed it away.

"Everyone thinks I'm crazy," she said.

"You're not crazy," Jessica said, standing nearby. "Your father has the same thing."

Katie looked at me with pleading eyes. "What is she talking about?" she asked.

"I have a lot to tell you," I said, trying to break it to her slowly. "For now, just trust us. What you're going through can be explained."

"Why don't we all go home and talk?" Jessica suggested.

Katie nodded and got up from the bench. She walked toward the parking lot and Jessica followed closely behind. I started to go after them when I felt my phone buzz in my pocket. I looked at the display screen and saw a number I hadn't seen in eight years. It was one I hoped I would never see again. Agent Charles Linden of the FBI.

Chapter Three

I had worked with Agent Linden several years earlier on a case involving a highly delusional serial killer and was still recovering from the effects it had on my psyche, not to mention my family. I hesitated before answering and, despite Jessica impatiently beckoning me toward the parking lot, clicked the "Talk" button on my cell phone and waved them to go on ahead.

"Hello, Agent Linden," I said.

"How have you been, Max?" he asked.

"Busy," I said. "Is there something I can help you with?"

"Cutting right to the chase," he said coyly. "I always liked that about you, Max. I need your help. There's a woman someone tried to murder and you're the only one that might be able to get some answers."

"I'm sure you have plenty of qualified people that could interview her. Why me?"

"Because she's in a coma. She was severely beaten, but, as fate would have it, didn't die."

"Jesus. Is she going to recover?"

"They're not sure at this point, but, God forbid, she doesn't, we're going to need to act quickly. I thought maybe you could get inside her head and find out who did it to her."

"Who is this woman?"

"I can only disclose if you're going to commit. I know about the prison, Max. I'm sorry."

"Apparently word gets around pretty quickly," I said, smiling at Jessica and holding up a finger to indicate "one more minute." "Look, I'll have to call you back, okay? Things are kind of hectic right now."

"Of course," he said. "You have my number. Just let me know as soon as you decide. She may not have much time left."

After I got off the phone, I went home, and Jessica and I had a long talk with Katie at our kitchen table. She listened avidly as we explained the nature of psychic phenomena, how I'd discovered I had abilities at a younger age than her and detailed the work I'd been doing at the prison since she was a kid. Expecting a myriad of questions afterwards, Katie started with one that a lot of teenagers would've probably asked.

"Can I move shit with my mind?" she inquired excitedly.

"Katie!" Jessica scolded her. "Watch your language!"

"What?!" Katie acted innocent. "It's a fair question!"

"No," I answered. "You can't move *things* with your mind."

"Well, that sucks," she said. "What about controlling other people's thoughts?!"

"Nope," I said, shaking my head. "I'm afraid that's off the table as well."

She threw her hands in the air. "So, then what's the point?! I just have to hear what other people are thinking and do nothing?!"

"Well..." I continued. "We were hoping you might use it for something good one day."

"Like your father," Jessica interjected.

"Booooring," she said and got up from the table. "This is a lot to process. May I please be excused?"

"Of course," I said. "But if you have any more questions—"

"I know," she interrupted. "I'll come and ask you guys."

She took off toward her room. I watched as she cut through the living room and down the hallway. I'd seen her scamper off in that direction many times before, only now she was taller and a whole lot sassier. Jessica sighed and got up from her chair. She moved to the counter near the sink and turned on the coffee pot. She took a bag of French roast out of a cabinet directly above her head.

"You never used to drink coffee," I commented.

"Gotta keep up with the five-year-olds," she said.

Teaching hadn't aged Jessica a bit. She was still as beautiful as the day we met, unaffected by the passage of time and its many tolls. I, on the other hand, seemed to find a new wrinkle every time I looked in the mirror. I watched dazedly as she made coffee, her shapely figure filling out a long, flowing, flowery dress. She seemed out of place in our mundane kitchen.

"They're shutting the program down at the prison," I announced matter-of-factly. "In one week, I'll be out of a job."

She turned away from the coffee pot and looked at me. "Oh, Max. I'm sorry. I know how much it meant to you."

I shrugged. "I did it for fourteen years," I said. "Maybe it's time to do something different."

"Well, it's not like we need the money," she said. "We've saved so much over the years you could practically retire."

"Or…" I began. "I could work in another capacity."

"Like what?" she said, sitting down at the table across from me.

"That call earlier…it was Agent Linden."

"Oh, Jesus. *Him* again? What did he want?"

"He wants me to help him with a case. A woman was badly beaten and is now in a coma."

"Oh, my God."

"He wants me to enter her mind and find out who did it," I continued.

"Have you ever gone into a coma patient's mind before? I thought you only did dreams."

I shook my head. "It might not even work, but, if there's a chance, it may be worth a shot."

"Okay, but does it have to be with him? The last time things got pretty ugly. I don't want any of us to have to go through that again."

"And we wouldn't. Look, I don't like him either. But what good is having psychic abilities if I don't use them to help somebody?"

She reached out and took my hand. "You know I'll support you no matter what you decide," she said. "I just want you to be careful."

What I hadn't told Jessica was that I had entered one of the inmates' minds during a moment of unconsciousness outside of normal sleep. His name was Arnold Greasey and he had

Matthew Franks

been incarcerated for armed robbery and assault with a deadly weapon. One day, I was walking through the prison grounds when Arnold and another prisoner got into an argument over a third prisoner and which of them he "belonged to." The argument escalated into violence when the second inmate knocked Arnold to the ground and proceeded to ram his head into concrete repeatedly.

By the time the guards intervened, Arnold wasn't moving. They pulled the other inmate off him and dragged him away. After contacting the infirmary to come and get Arnold, I leaned down beside him and checked his vitals. He was still breathing, albeit shallowly, and his heartbeat was steady. I said his name several times and asked if he could hear me, but he was unresponsive.

A small crowd had gathered at that point and, once the medic arrived, Arnold was laid out on a stretcher. I helped take him to the infirmary and stood by as a doctor and nurse did what they could to help him. His heartbeat suddenly slowed, and the doctor and nurse acted more quickly. Wanting to help in some way, I entered Arnold's mind while they were occupied to wake him up from inside.

Once in his mind, however, I found myself in a dark room surrounded by what seemed like thousands of luminescent butterflies. They swarmed around me and picked me up off the ground. As we ascended toward the ceiling of the room, I noticed my reflection in one of their wings. I was no longer myself. I was Arnold Greasey. Seconds later, I was jolted out of Arnold's mind and back into the infirmary. Despite the doctors' and nurses' efforts, Arnold was dead.

After that, I developed an interest in the mind moments before death. I didn't get another opportunity to experience it firsthand but researched it quite a bit. I discovered there were more questions than answers, not to mention the fact there was no way to follow up with a subject once he was gone, and decided to move on to something more accessible. When Linden called about the coma patient, my interest was piqued once again. Obviously, I didn't want the woman to die but couldn't help but wonder what I might uncover in such a state.

Katie abruptly appeared in the kitchen. "I have more questions," she said with a serious look on her face. "Can I turn it off?" she asked.

"No," I told her honestly. "But you will learn to control it so that it doesn't control you."

She nodded. "Can I tell my friends?"

"Definitely not," Jessica answered. "This doesn't leave this room, okay?"

"Fine," she said.

"I'm not kidding, Katie. If the public finds out, they'd never leave us alone. Your father only let the CIA know and, thank God, we've been able to keep it a secret this long. Promise us you won't say anything to anyone."

"I promise," she said with the same innocent look on her face she had when she was four and promised she wouldn't take cookies from the pantry without asking. She plopped down in a chair between us at the table. "What's for dinner?" she asked nonchalantly.

A short while later, I stepped out and into our backyard and called Linden. He was, as I expected, stingy with the details. The woman, Beth Martin, had spent the weekend in rural Kentucky at her parents' house and was driving back home to Louisville late at night. A truck driver noticed her abandoned car on the side of the road and called the police. Her parents and fiancé were contacted, and, after an exhaustive search of the surrounding area, she was found lying unconscious in a field a half a mile from where her vehicle was discovered.

"Did anybody see anything?" I asked.

"Nope," replied Linden. "It all happened on a farm road in the middle of the night. There was no one around."

"Was anything stolen?"

"Her purse was missing from the car," he answered. "According to her parents, she didn't carry cash around with her, so it was mainly credit cards and a few makeup items."

"Any fingerprints? Evidence?"

"No fingerprints," he said. "As for evidence, whoever did it took it with them. They found DNA samples that match her parents but that could've been from hugging her before she left their house. Other than that, it's all inconclusive."

"How did the parents seem?" I asked, looking in through the window at Jessica as she cooked dinner and then Katie at the kitchen table doing homework.

"Distraught. Beth is their only child."

"I can't even imagine," I said. "And the fiancé?"

"He won't talk to anybody, but he's been visiting her at the hospital. They were supposed to be married in April."

"Is there anyone that had it out for her? Somebody at work maybe?"

"We don't even know if was premeditated. It could've been some thug that was going to rape her and changed his mind at the last minute."

"So, she wasn't..."

"No. There were no signs of penetration and her clothing was intact."

"Thank God for that."

"Well, what do you say, Max?" he cut to the chase. "Can I put you on a plane to Louisville in the morning? All expenses paid, of course."

"I've only got a week to finish up things at the prison—"

"I'll get you an extension," he said assuredly. If there was one thing I didn't miss about Linden, it was his cockiness. "Just say the word and I'll get the ball rolling on my end."

"Yes," I said as Jessica beckoned me through the window to come in for dinner.

Chapter Four

The next morning, I told Jessica and Katie bye then drove an hour to the Houston airport.

I boarded a 9 a.m. flight to Louisville and arrived in the city shortly after 12:15 p.m. local time. I'd been to Kentucky once before as a child with my parents, primarily to fulfill my father's Civil War obsession, and remembered seeing a show about Stephen Foster, the nineteenth-century songwriter that penned notable tunes like "Oh! Susanna" and "My Old Kentucky Home." I learned later in life that the latter was an anti-slavery ballad involving a slave that had been taken from his home and longed to return one day.

I got off the plane, retrieved my luggage, and saw a driver standing close by with a sign that said "Crawford." I introduced myself and, without saying a word, he led me outside to a town car. I hopped into the back seat, and he drove me to the hotel in Louisville where I'd be staying. When I arrived, Linden was waiting for me outside, smoking a cigarette and talking on his phone. The driver retrieved my suitcase and carried it inside to the lobby.

"Yes ma'am," Linden said, nodding to acknowledge me as I walked toward him. "He just got into town. Oh, no. You don't need to go the trouble. Okay. One moment and I'll ask him."

He moved the phone away from his face. "Do you like blueberry pie?"

I shrugged. "I suppose," I told him.

"It's a simple question, Crawford. Do you like it or not?"

"Yes," I answered, resisting the urge to smack him thirty seconds into our first encounter in eight years.

"He does," he spoke into the phone again. "We'll be there in an hour, ma'am. See you then." He ended the call and then gave me a once-over. "Nice outfit," he said, motioning to my plaid shirt and khaki slacks. "Did you just come from a church picnic?"

"When did you start smoking?" I asked, ignoring him.

"Don't ask," he said, flicking the cigarette onto the ground. "Come on." He started toward a black luxury town car. "We'll take my rental."

"Where are we going?" I asked.

"To talk to Beth's parents," he replied. "They want to meet you first."

I motioned to the hotel. "Shouldn't I check in?"

"It's already been done. Your things will be in your room when we get back."

The drive to the home of Edward and Allie Martin took a little over an hour, primarily because we had to stop while a few cows crossed the road. Once out of Louisville, we were in farm country, the open fields and barns of rural America that thanklessly provided crops and livestock for cities too overcrowded for such endeavors. By the time we reached the Martins' ranch-style house and farm, I couldn't tell them apart from all the others we had passed along the way.

We drove up a gravel road to the main house and got out of the car. It was so quiet and peaceful that I suddenly felt very tired. I noticed a hammock near the back porch, and it began to call to me. Its summoning was crudely interrupted, however, when Agent Linden stepped in between us.

"You awake, Crawford?" he asked bluntly.

"I'm fine," I told him.

Mr. and Mrs. Martin stepped out onto the front porch of the house to greet us. Allie Martin had been a homemaker her whole adult life, the kind that went out of her way to be a hostess despite the fact something horrible had happened. Her silver hair shone in the sunlight as she made her way down the steps toward us. Edward, a lifetime farmer, followed slowly behind.

"Good afternoon," Allie spoke in a high pitch that betrayed her somber countenance.

"Nice to see you again, Agent Linden."

"Nice to see you, ma'am," he replied.

"You must be Mr. Crawford," she said, extending her hand.

"Pleased to meet you, Mrs. Martin," I said, accepting her handshake. Her grip was weak but warm. "I'm very sorry about your daughter."

"Thank you," she said, letting go. She motioned to Edward. "This is my husband, Edward. Edward, this is the man I told you about. He's here to find out what happened to Beth."

"I hope you can help our little girl," he said, avoiding eye contact.

"I'll do my best, sir," I said, trying to sound reassuring.

"We appreciate your efforts," said Allie. "Shall we go inside?"

We followed them into the house and I immediately felt like I had walked into an episode of *Little House on the Prairie*. Save the flat screen television mounted on the wall, the living room could've easily been a replica of one from a hundred years ago. Made up of handcrafted wooden furniture and a solid oak coffee table, it had a simplicity to it that had long been squelched by modern day design. There was even an old mahogany desk with an oil lamp on it in the corner of the room where I imagined Mr. Martin wrote letters on parchment with a long-feathered quill pen.

"Please have a seat," Allie said, motioning to a couch with hand-stitched pillows I assumed she had made herself. "I'll get the blueberry pie," she added and then left to enter the kitchen.

Taking the lead, Linden sat down first, and I eased onto the couch next to him. Edward sat down in a rocking chair, which not surprisingly, was right next to a fireplace stacked with wood. I imagined the two of them sitting together on a cold, winter night as the flames crackled and warmed them up late into the evening. For a long time, Edward didn't say anything. I tried reading his mind, but it was scrambled. Little seemingly unrelated thoughts would pop in his head only to quickly dissipate. For example, he abruptly went from wondering how old Linden and I were to reminding himself to feed the chickens.

"Here we are," Allie said, entering the room and placing the best blueberry pie I'd ever seen on the coffee table. It was on a silver tray along with silverware and four small plates. "Go on," she said, sitting in a matching love seat across from us. "Don't be shy."

"Thank you," I said, reaching for a spatula tucked under a particularly tasty-looking piece. "It's very nice of you."

Linden gave me a look as I put a piece on one of the plates, but I didn't care. I had missed breakfast, so homemade blueberry pie sounded amazing. I took a bite and had to stop myself from letting out a low moan. I placed the plate on the table, careful not to scarf down the whole thing at once. I restrained myself despite the smell wafting up into my nose and taking hold of me like a spell.

"It's delicious," I told Allie.

"I'm glad you like it," she said.

Linden sighed. "Mr. and Mrs. Martin," he began impatiently. "Is there anything you can tell Mr. Crawford about that night that might help him, some type of clue maybe?"

Allie shook her head. "Not really," she replied. "Beth came in for the weekend like she always does from time to time. She said it was to get away from the city, but I know it's that job of hers at the art gallery. Very stressful. She stayed late Sunday night and headed home around nine. Or was it ten?"

"Sleeping pills," Edward blurted out.

"Excuse me?" said Linden.

"My wife takes sleeping pills," Edward continued. "That could be why she don't remember."

"Now Edward, I'm sure these young men don't need to know about that."

"Actually, it could helpful," said Linden. "Did you take sleeping pills that night?"

"Yes," she replied hesitantly. "I take them every night. They help me...wind down before bed."

"What time do you take them?"

"Around eight thirty."

"Do you remember Beth leaving that night, Mrs. Martin?"

"I'm sorry, but I'm afraid I don't. I told her goodnight and went to bed. It wasn't until later that night that Edward woke me up when the police called."

"So, are you some kind of mind reader?" Edward suddenly

asked me. "Like Johnny Carson when he played that fellow with the turban?"

"Not exactly," I said, grinning. "I'm more of a face-to-face kind of mind reader."

"You'll have to excuse my husband," said Allie. "We had Beth later in life after we decided we couldn't have children. It was a miracle really. I was forty-four and Edward was forty-seven. Now we're in our seventies, and sometimes our minds aren't as focused as they used to be."

"It's fine," I said.

"What about her fiancé?" Linden jumped back in. "What was he doing earlier that evening?"

"You'll have to ask him," Allie said. "He's at the hospital with Beth now."

Linden nodded. "Anything else you can tell us?" he asked. "Was Beth acting differently that night?"

"No different than any other time," answered Allie. "Like I said, she has a stressful job. As much as she likes coming here, she's always rushing to get back home. It's like she suddenly realizes she has a deadline or something."

"I see," said Linden. "Well, with your permission, we'd like to go to the hospital now and let Mr. Crawford see if he can find out anything."

"You have our permission," she said. "At this point, we're open to almost anything." She looked at me intently. "You're going to go into her head?" she asked.

"Yes," I answered.

"When you're in there, please tell her we love her."

"Of course," I told her even though I had no idea what was in store for me.

After I finished the pie, I gave Mrs. Martin my phone number and asked her to call me if she thought of anything else that might be helpful. Then Linden and I left and headed back to Louisville. Upon our arrival at the hospital, a nurse escorted us to Beth's room. I peeked in through the window from the hallway and saw her lying there, all peaceful and quiet. No sooner than the nurse opened the door, Bobby Fugate, Beth's fiancé, blocked our entrance.

"I'm not going to allow this," he said to Linden without even glancing at me. "Who the hell do you think you are bringing some quack to see my fiancée?"

Bobby was in his early thirties and dressed like he was running for Congress. His immaculate suit and tie were overshadowed only by his two-hundred-dollar haircut. He reminded me of Linden in a way but more aggressive and potentially way more annoying. I stepped aside so the near-doppelgängers could hash it out.

"You don't have any say in the matter, Mr. Fugate," Linden told him authoritatively.

"Beth's mom and dad agreed to it."

"I don't care!" he said. "They're too old to be making decisions like this! I should be able to say 'no' to this nonsense! I'm going to be her husband!"

"Of course, you are," Linden said smugly. "But you're not yet. Now if you'd be so kind as to step aside, we have work to do. Unless you're planning to interfere with a federal investigation, in which case you could face charges."

Bobby glared at Linden for a minute but ultimately backed down. "This is bullshit!" he said and then brushed past me on his way out of the room.

"I take it he's not open to questions," I said.

"Don't worry about him," Linden said. "I'll wait outside and make sure nobody comes in. We can debrief afterwards. Do you need anything before you get started?"

"No." I entered the room and saw Beth up-close for the first time. "Let's just hope it works."

Chapter Five

After my initial visit into Beth's unconscious, I realized I needed to get creative if I was going to make any headway. Not only was she in a place that seemed to offer her escape, but she also thought she was someone named Margaret Stevens, a person I hadn't heard of before. The truth was I required assistance, and, since I couldn't bring anyone in with me, I opted to become the ones in Beth's life that might be able to help. More succinctly, I decided to practice the art of shapeshifting.

Transforming into others within dreams is one of the techniques I learned during the later years of working at the prison. Early on, I had no clue what I was capable of but, through trial and error, discovered little tricks I could use to help rehabilitate an inmate.

In the case of Donald Thatcher, the one thing that made him conscious of the horrible nature of his crime was his grandmother or, for therapeutic purposes, me masquerading as his grandmother.

At the age of eighteen, still living at home, Donald got into an argument with his parents over how much time he spent in his room playing video games. Ultimately, Donald's father took the gaming device out of his room and gave him an ultimatum. Either he got a job, or he had to move out of the house. This made Donald very angry. So much so that, mimicking the style of one his favorite games involving a covert assassin, he snuck into his parents' room in the middle of the night and slit their throats.

When Donald went to prison, his eighty-year-old grandmother was the only person that would visit him. She'd bring him cookies, see how he was doing, but never once confronted him about killing her son and daughter-in-law. Not surprisingly, Donald loved when she came to see him and entered a depression when she passed away two years into his sentence. I started working with him about six months after her death.

At first, Donald wanted nothing to do with me. When I went into his dreams, he'd try to kill me off with an imaginary sword or flamethrower. Obviously, he couldn't hurt me, but I still gave him the satisfaction of "getting rid of me" by disappearing from his dreams.

After all, there's no use hanging around if the person you're trying to help isn't ready to be helped yet.

But then I had a potentially unethical yet promising hypothesis. If I were to confront Donald as his grandmother, would he be more likely to feel remorse for his crime and stand a better chance of being rehabilitated? Nothing else was working so I figured it was worth a shot. I began experimenting with self-morphing inside my own dreams. I even studied home movies of Donald's grandmother to learn her mannerisms and voice patterns. I had already been mentally projecting objects into dreams so I decided changing my appearance couldn't be that much more difficult. I was wrong.

As it turns out, using your mind to alter yourself into someone else requires a keen sense of detail and razor-sharp concentration. One false move and you completely blow your cover.

For example, the first time I tried it in one of Donald's dreams, I accidentally thought of my dog Spots I had as a kid and morphed into Donald's grandmother's body but with Spots' head.

Luckily, Donald didn't see me, and I was able to try again.

Once I was finally able to accurately portray his grandmother, Donald no longer tried to kill me. I had his complete attention. I told him he had done a bad thing but that I still loved him.

He broke down into tears that subsequently continued when he woke up in the prison mental health wing where I had projected into his dream through a one-way mirror. Not long after that, he was open to treatment for the first time and has been making progress ever since.

In Beth Martin's case, I didn't have a specific person in mind. My goal was to try different people in her life and see who caused a reaction. Since she identified herself as Margaret during our first encounter, my hope was that someone close to her might remind her of her true identity and, thus, bring her out of the false one. I decided to start with her parents since I'd had some, albeit brief, interactions with them.

After settling myself into the visitor's chair in her hospital room, I projected into her mind for the second time and, once again, landed in the middle of the golf course at her imaginary "retirement" hotel. In the distance, I saw her sitting on the veranda at the same table as before and slipped out of sight behind a tree. I focused on the details of Allie Martin's face, the dress she wore the day we met, and the Southern drawl when she spoke. I stepped out from behind the tree and made my way to the veranda. When I reached her table, she was staring at the ground.

"Hello, honey," I said, doing my best to sound motherly. "How are you doing?"

She looked up at me and paused for a moment. She studied me the way you study a person you sort of recognize but can't quite place from where. Wanting to help jog her memory further, I took the seat across from her and placed my hand on hers. She looked at my hand and then back at me. Before I could say anything else, she suddenly pulled her hand away from mine.

"What's wrong with you?" she asked.

"I thought you might want to talk," I answered.

"Why would I talk to you?" she said. "I don't even know you."

I nodded. "I'm sorry I bothered you," I said and then got up from the table.

I walked away and sat down at an unoccupied table on the far side of the veranda.

I made sure I was well out of sight when I quickly and quietly transformed into Edward Martin.

I stood and moved back toward Beth, going much slower this time to replicate her father's deliberate and controlled gait. When I reached her table, she looked up and smiled warmly at me.

"You're a little early. Aren't you?" she said.

"Am I?" I asked in his deep voice, feeling optimistic. "I thought I was on time."

"I'm afraid not. Bingo doesn't start until six."

"Bingo?"

"That is what you're here for. Isn't it?"

"Of course," I said, my hopes dashed. "Bingo. I'll come back later."

"Good idea," she said, grinning. "You take care of yourself now."

"You too," I said and then stepped away from her table once again.

I wandered off to another part of the veranda and sat down. So far, I was oh for two with only one shot left. She didn't recognize her parents, or at least acted like she didn't, so when I changed into her fiancé, I was expecting a similar response. I got up, walked over to her table and sat down across from her. To my surprise, she grabbed my hands and pulled me toward her.

"Where have you been?" she said and then kissed me on the lips. "I've been waiting forever."

I froze. Not only was I not anticipating a reaction, but I certainly wasn't prepared for such a strong one. A million thoughts went through my head at that moment, but, first and foremost, I pictured Jessica sitting at the table next to us. She wasn't speaking, just giving me a look as if to say "Really? Kissing coma patients in their dreams? Are you kidding me right now?"

"I'm sorry," I said, pulling away from Beth but trying not to be too obvious. "I didn't know you were waiting for me."

"Well, who else would I be waiting for, silly?" she said, leaning in for another kiss.

This time, I turned my face away and her lips landed on my cheek. I had two options at that point. Either get the hell out of there or try to understand why she recognized her fiancé but not her parents. Opting to stay, I reminded myself that I had to be very careful how I acted with Beth. One false move and I could blow the whole operation. She let go of my hands and gave me a bewildered look.

"What's wrong?" she asked. "Aren't you glad to see me?"

"Of course," I said. "I'm just…not feeling well. I think I may be coming down with the flu."

"Oh, you poor baby," she said, reaching across the table and touching my cheek. "You do feel a little cold. What do you say we go back to our room and take a nice, warm bath? I bet that'll make you feel better."

"Room?" I looked toward the entrance into the inside of the "resort." "You have a room here?"

She giggled. "Of course," she said. "You're the one that booked it, you goofball. You must not be feeling well if you can't even remember that!" She stood and gently pulled me to my feet. "Tell you what," she said. "Why don't we go to the room and lie down for a while? Maybe a little rest will do you some good."

"Okay," I said, only agreeing to it because she was potentially leading me to a part of her mind where there were more clues.

"Come on then," she said, taking my hand.

She led me through the restaurant area and to the door leading inside. When she opened it, I assumed we'd enter the high school classroom from my first visit, but we walked straight into the lobby instead. Why the classroom was there before and gone now I had no idea, but more importantly, did my presence masquerading as Beth's fiancé Bobby have anything to do with its disappearance? The sounds of ballroom music played in the lobby at a low volume.

"Ah, yes," a voice came from behind us. I turned to see that it was the waiter that had previously facilitated my removal. "The lovebirds," he continued. "Will you be dining in your room this evening?"

"I'm afraid not, Sammy," Beth said, patting me on the stomach. "It seems the little baby has a tummy ache."

"Ewww," said Sammy, holding his nose in the air aristocratically. Then he addressed me. "Do mind the carpet, will you? It takes weeks to get human vomit stains out of it."

Sammy walked off in another direction. I was watching to see where he was going when something far more interesting caught my eye. The half-human, half-alien "security guards" were back. Only this time they were dancing in the middle of the lobby. Their tentacles intertwined, the two strange, inexplicable creatures waltzed up and down the floor to the ballroom music.

Beth linked her arm with mine. "Aren't they beautiful?" she asked.

"What are they exactly?" I inquired.

"You must be sick!" she said and then cuddled up to me. "We made them together. Don't you remember?"

"Of course," I said, playing along. "Remind me of their names again."

"That one is Grilax," she said, pointing to one of them. "And that one is Grulax," she added, pointing to the other one. "Now come on." She nudged me toward a hallway off the lobby. "Let's get you feeling better."

We walked down what seemed like a normal hotel hallway except for one key difference.

The room numbers were out of order. As we made our way to the end of the corridor, I noticed a familiar pattern of numbers on the doors. 2-6-7-21-31. It was the same sequence of numbers on the chalkboard in the high school classroom I'd seen before. The series repeated until we reached the last room on the left. It said "31" at the top of the door. Directly under the number was a piece of expensive-looking stationery stuck to the door. On the stationery, written in elegant calligraphy, were the words "Mr. and Mrs. Stevens."

"Here we are," Beth said and then opened the door. A blinding bright light emanated from the room. She motioned for me to go in first. "After you, Mr. Sick Pants."

I shielded my eyes from the light and cautiously stepped inside.

Chapter Six

The inside of the room looked like a standard double bed hotel suite, but, bathed in the extremely bright light, seemed ethereal. Still halfway covering my eyes, I saw a sleepaway couch across from a flat screen television perched on a small table. Beth walked past them and into the part of the suite with the beds. She turned to me and smiled. The overwhelming luminescence enveloped her, making her appear angelic.

"Well, don't just stand there," she said. "Take off your clothes and get in bed."

"Do you think we could turn the lights down a little?" I asked.

"Of course," she said, moving to a knob on the wall. She turned it to the left and the lighting became normal and much more bearable. "Is that better?" she asked.

"Yes," I answered. "Thank you."

She sat on one of the beds and patted the bedspread next to her. "Come on," she said. "Do you want me to help you get undressed?" she added with a sly smile.

"That's okay."

She frowned. "You're no fun," she said.

"Sorry," I said, noticing the door to the bathroom was closed. "I need to use the restroom."

"Okay, but, when you come back, you'd better be naked. I know I'll be."

She winked at me. I nodded and forced a grin. I opened the door to the bathroom to find that it was pitch-black inside. I couldn't see a toilet or bathtub or anything. I felt along the wall for a light switch but there wasn't one. I stepped in and closed the door. Suddenly, an older, shabbily dressed man holding a lit torch was standing in front of me. I quickly realized we were inside a cave.

"Do you know the password?" he asked impatiently.

"Password?"

He sighed. "I can't take you any farther without the password." He motioned to the door behind me. "Off you go," he said and then disappeared into thin air.

Trying to process everything, I opened the door and stepped back into the hotel suite. I didn't hear anything in the bedroom area but anticipated the need to cover my eyes if Beth was in a state of undress. I cautiously moved forward, only to find that she was gone. I looked around the room, under the bed, and in the closet, but there was no sign of her. Just as I was about to leave, some reddish goo plopped down on my forehead. I tilted my head back to see a crimson-colored creature sticking to the ceiling with webbed feet and hands.

The creature pounced on me and threw me to the ground. It leapt on top of me and started choking me. I got a good look at its face. It had the same huge, black eyes and sharp-toothed mouth as the creature back in the high school classroom during my first visit to Beth's unconscious mind. I also noticed that it had breasts, but they were covered in hair. Not wanting to harm the creature, I carefully pulled its hands away from my throat and got to my feet. I pushed the creature against the wall. It wasn't difficult to subdue but it let out a high-pitched yelp that seemed to last for an eternity. I just stood there, restraining it, until it finally stopped.

Defeated, the creature fell forward into my arms. I laid it down gently onto one of the beds and it curled into a fetal position. It then transformed into Beth. I pulled the blanket down to cover her naked body.

"Are you alright?" I asked.

"Just go," she whispered, not looking at me.

"Are you sure?"

"Go!" she shouted. "Leave me alone!"

I backed away from the bed and moved to the door. I opened the door and stepped outside, wanting to give her the impression I was merely leaving the room instead of abruptly disappearing when I withdrew from her mind. I shut the door and checked both ways down the hallway to make sure the coast was clear before exiting. Once I was certain no one was around, I transformed back into myself. Right as I was about to pull out of Beth's unconsciousness, a nine- or ten-year-old girl appeared out of nowhere and startled me.

"Jesus!" I said, taken aback. "Where did you come from?"

She pointed to a nearby room with the number "7" on the door. Wearing a simple, light blue dress with a white bow tied in the front and a barrette in her hair, she reminded me of one of the twins from *The Shining*. The fact we were standing in what seemed like an eternally long hotel hallway wasn't helping matters. In spite of the eeriness, I crouched down to her height level and forced a smile.

"What's your name?" I asked.

"Elizabeth," she answered. "What's yours?"

"My name is Max," I said, extending my hand. "It's nice to meet you."

She reluctantly shook my hand. "Are you a stranger?" she asked, letting go. "My mommy and daddy told me to never talk to strangers."

"And right they were to tell you that. No, I'm not a stranger. I know your mom and dad." I motioned to the room with the "7" on it. "Are they in the room?"

"No," she said. "They went to town."

"Oh? Are you by yourself?"

"Yes. Can I show you something?"

"Of course."

She took me by the hand and led me to the room. She opened the door and coaxed me inside. The second we crossed the threshold, we were transported to the house where Beth's parents lived. We were standing on the same front porch I had stood on during my actual visit.

Curious as to how the inside of the house looked in her psyche, I moved toward the door. She pulled me away from it.

"It's not in there," she said. "Come on. I'll show you."

She led me down the steps and around the back of the

house. The property seemed to stretch for miles even though it was only twenty acres in reality. A cornfield took up quite a bit of space, but there were also gardens growing tomatoes, peas, and peppers. A few lazy cows grazed on grass nearby, and a chicken coop occupied a small piece of land perpendicular to the house. However, this wasn't the view Little Beth wanted me to see. She coaxed me to the back porch and motioned to the three-foot-tall crawlspace underneath the wood floor.

"It's under there," she said.

I slowly moved forward, halfway expecting her alternate demon-self to come leaping out from under the porch. Bracing myself, I crouched down to see what she down there. In the alternating pattern of light and dark caused by the sun creeping in through the spaces between the wooden boards of the porch floor, I saw the decomposing body of a dog, wasting away and being eaten by a swarm of maggots.

I instinctively covered my mouth and nose to avoid the smell. Remembering it wasn't real, I lowered my hand and turned to Little Beth. She was holding a bloody knife in one hand and a rusted shovel in the other. Whereas the sky above us had been a beautiful clear blue seconds before, it had shifted to an ominous black. She inched toward me with the knife and shovel with a grave look on her face.

"I didn't mean to do it," she said. "It was an accident, I swear. Will you help me bury him before Mommy and Daddy get home? They'll be mad at me if they find out."

"What happened?" I asked, keeping my distance.

"I was just playing with the knife. I didn't mean for it to go in. I put him under there to hide him but he's starting to stink. Will you please help me?"

Not knowing if intervening would help or hinder the investigative process, I had to make a quick decision. My goal was to get Beth to trust me so that I could learn as many details about the case as possible. Nevertheless, I needed to be cautious or else I could potentially alter actual memories that could be useful in piecing the puzzle together. Realizing there was no way to determine the best solution, I opted to assist Little Beth in burying the rotting carcass of the unfortunate canine.

"Okay," I said, reaching out to take the shovel. "Where should we bury him?"

She pointed to a specific area about thirty yards from the back porch. "There," she said.

"Will you carry him?" she asked. "I don't want to get my dress dirty."

"Sure," I agreed hesitantly. "What was the dog's name?"

"Petey," she answered with a sad look on her face.

I peeked under the porch floor at the poor creature. It reminded me of a Cocker Spaniel named "Corky" I had when I was a kid. I loved that dog. He would meet me at the front door every day after school and put his paw out to shake hands. And then one day my parents told me Corky "ran away." Even though I didn't believe them, I didn't dare ask what really happened. I figured if they had to lie, it must've been pretty bad.

I laid the shovel by the side of the house and crouched low to avoid bumping my head on the wood floor. I tried swatting away the maggots but could only rid myself of half of the mob. I reached under the belly of the dead animal and hoisted it up into my arms. One of its legs fell off onto the ground. I leaned down, careful not to drop any other parts, picked up the leg, and then carried the remains out into the dark light of day.

I followed Little Beth to the piece of land she had indicated and carefully set Petey down beside her. I went back and grabbed the shovel, all the while wondering if my parents had secretly buried Corky in our backyard while I was ignorantly playing over at a friend's house.

I carried the shovel over to where Beth was standing, and she pointed to an exact spot a few feet away from Petey.

"Right there," she said.

I pushed the shovel into the soft earth with my foot and threw the dirt to the side. I uncovered the soil a few more times, making a small pile to cover Petey once I lowered him into the hole. Only the next time I went to dig, I noticed there was nothing left to displace. Instead, there was a portal into outer space. Whereas above us the sky was dark and threatening, below us everything was calm and peaceful. The moon and stars were in plain view through the opening, closer than I had ever seen them before.

"Put him in, please," Little Beth said, sniffling.

I carefully picked up Petey and moved him into the bottomless hole. I let go of him and watched as his decaying, lifeless body floated away. The maggots separated from him and slowly spiraled off into different directions like some demented ballet. Petey drifted further, eventually receding into the distance and disappearing into the cosmos. I turned to Little Beth and saw that she was crying. I gently placed my hand on her shoulder.

"It's okay," I said, trying to console her. I reached my free hand out toward the bloody knife. "May I have that?" I asked.

She nodded and gave it to me. "I really didn't mean to do it," she said sobbing. "He was such a good dog. He always wanted to play. Am I a bad person?"

"No," I told her. "Bad people don't have remorse for their actions. You obviously cared about him." I thought of Corky again. "Just try to remember all the fun times you had together."

She looked up at me and smiled. "Thank you," she said, wiping her eyes.

"You're welcome," I said, tears welling up in mine.

Chapter Seven

Agent Linden didn't have an office to use temporarily at the hospital, so we sat in his car in the parking lot as he smoked a cigarette out the partially cracked driver-side window. True to form, he listened to everything I'd experienced in Beth's mind with a look of smug skepticism on his face. He was like that one guy at the magic show that wanted to be sure everyone around him knew he wasn't going to have the wool pulled over his eyes.

"So, let me get this straight," he said, blowing smoke in more ways than one. "Her older self thinks she's someone else, but her younger self said her name was Elizabeth?"

"Yes."

"How the hell does that happen?"

"It could be that the trauma of the attack somehow set her back emotionally. Maybe she feels more comfortable being her younger self because she isn't ready to deal with it. There was a teenage version of her too, but I haven't talked to that one yet."

"Jesus, Crawford. Can't you just get her to be one version of herself? The one that can tell us who tried to murder her?"

"It's not that easy."

"Well, have you had inmates do something like this in their dreams?"

"Sure."

"What'd you do then?"

"It was different. Sometimes they would pretend to be someone else just to forget about their crimes for a while. But they knew they were pretending. I think Beth really believes she's someone else."

"Well, you'll just have to convince her that she's not. Now

what about the fiancé? You said he was the only one she recognized."

"But not as Bobby Fugate. As Mr. Stevens. It would help if I could talk to him."

"But there is no Mr. Stevens."

"I meant Fugate."

"I doubt he'll talk to you. He already made a statement. Unless he becomes a suspect, he doesn't have to say another word."

As it turned out, Bobby Fugate had an alibi for the night Beth was nearly killed. After a long night of boozing it up with the senior members of his law firm, he returned home to his inner-city apartment allegedly expecting Beth to be there. When she was nowhere to be found, he tried reaching her on her cell phone, a call that was made approximately two hours after the attack would've taken place. He then drove to his future in-laws' farm house and Beth was discovered early the next morning.

"I still need to try," I said. "Where's his law office?"

"About two miles from here," replied Linden.

"Can we go there?"

"It'll piss him off, so absolutely."

Linden started the engine and we drove out of the hospital parking lot. Within a few minutes we were outside the Law Offices of Baxter, Freeman, and Lester. Linden crammed his car into a metered spot between two vehicles, nearly ramming one and then the other as he settled into place. From where we were sitting, I could see the Ohio River nearly a stone's throw away across the interstate. Directly on the other side was Indiana, a piece of geography I remembered from childhood but never expected to experience.

We got out of the car and walked up to the front door of the law office. Linden led the way inside and I followed close behind. There was a blonde-haired receptionist at a desk texting away on her cell phone. It was fairly easy to tell by the furniture in the waiting area that the firm had been successful. Not to mention the prime downtown office spot. The receptionist didn't look up from her phone.

"Can I help you?" she asked indifferently.

"We're here to see Bobby Fugate," Linden answered.

"Mr. Fugate is out of the office at the moment," the receptionist replied, still texting away. "Would you like to leave him a message?"

"Do you have any idea when he'll be back?" I asked.

"Nope," she said.

Just then the front door opened and an older man in a suit entered the office. He gave Linden and me a once-over. "Are you gentlemen seeking legal counsel?" he inquired.

"We're here to see Mr. Fugate," Linden told him. "Will he be in today?"

"I'm afraid not," the man answered. "He's in court all day. Is there something I can do for you?"

"Actually, maybe there is," I said. "My name's Max Crawford," I said, extending my hand.

The older man accepted hesitantly. "Oscar Freeman," he reciprocated.

I motioned to Linden. "This is Agent Linden of the FBI We're investigating the attack on Mr. Fugate's fiancée, Beth Martin. Do you know her?"

"Yes," he answered. "I know Beth. Lovely girl. It's a shame what happened to her. Why don't we go somewhere we can talk more privately?" He turned to the receptionist, who was now eavesdropping without trying to hide it. "Any messages for me, Candace?" he asked, giving her a disapproving look.

"No, Mr. Freeman," she replied, pretending to go back to work. "Nothing this morning."

"Thank you, Candace," he said. "This way, gentlemen."

He led us down a hallway and into a suite of offices. Each one had the name of each senior partner on gold plates on the door. I didn't see one for Fugate. Freeman brought us into a conference room with a long, mahogany table in the middle of it. There were several plush office chairs around the table. An unobstructed view of the Ohio River filled a window that ran the length of one of the walls. Freeman motioned to two of the chairs.

"Please, have a seat."

We sat down on the side facing the window and Freeman

took a chair at the head of the table. In the center of the table, there was a bouquet of flowers. Next to the bouquet, there was a box of tissues. I assumed they were for clients when they found out how much their bill was going to be. Freeman leaned back in his chair, obviously very comfortable in his senior position.

"I'm gonna level with you, gentlemen," he said with an air of authority. "Bobby's already told me about you and, frankly, I disagree with how you're handling the investigation. But it's not up to me, so here we are. How can I help you?"

"How long has Mr. Fugate worked for your firm?" I asked.

"This is his second year with us. He's in line to be partner one day. He's a very bright and driven young man. Kind of like me when I was his age."

I paused to read Freeman's mind. He genuinely liked Bobby. He even had feelings toward him as if he were his own son. Linden and I, on the other hand, Freeman did not like.

He was trying very hard to hide his disdain for us coming to his place of business in the middle of the day unannounced. As for Beth, he didn't seem to care one way or the other. He was very much about keeping up appearances.

"Any further questions?" he added with a grin that bared his teeth.

"Only a couple more," I said. "How did Bobby act after the attack?"

"What do you mean?"

"Was his ability to perform his duties affected? Did he ask for time off?"

"No, he did not. I encouraged him to take time off, but he insisted on continuing to work. He said he needed to stay busy to keep his mind off it. I'm sure you can both understand. As for his performance, he's as top notch as he's always been. Does that make him a suspect?"

"Should it?" asked Linden.

Freeman smiled. "I assure you Bobby loves Beth very much. He wants to find the person that did this to her even more than you do." He started to get up from his chair. "Now, if you gentlemen will excuse me—"

"Just one more question if you don't mind," I said.

"Of course not," he said, simultaneously sitting back down and wanting to punch me in the face. "Go right ahead."

"Can you think of any reason Bobby would want to impede our investigation?" I asked.

"Let's just cut to the chase, why don't we?" he said, no longer feigning a grin. "This psychic nonsense isn't helping anybody. Why don't you leave the poor girl alone? The truth always comes out one way or another. Why continue with this charade?"

"Her parents don't seem to think it's a charade," said Linden. "They actually want our help."

"Her father is losing his mind and her mother is so desperate she'll do anything," said Freeman. "Of course, they'll agree to the most cockamamie idea that comes their way. Why get their hopes up?"

"Because they deserve justice," answered Linden.

"Justice," Freeman scoffed. "That word is thrown around so often it's lost its meaning. What they deserve is closure."

Closure was a concept I always struggled with in my job. A respectable goal, no doubt, but one that seemed perpetually out of reach. Even when inmates came to terms with their crimes, were forgiven by their victims' families, and gave their life to God, the nightmares still came back. No example better illustrates the apparent inescapable nature of the past than Paul Fletcher, an inmate convicted of killing a man while driving intoxicated.

One wouldn't assume Paul Fletcher would be capable of such a thing. A very mild-mannered and polite man of fifty-seven, he served as assistant to the prison chaplain, a role he took very seriously when it came to converting other inmates. He also publicly confessed to his crime in front of his victim's surviving family members, a gesture that would eventually cause them to cease pursuing the death penalty for him. He felt true remorse for his crime, made amends to the best of his ability, and found solace in religion. One might even say he had atoned for his sins.

But, as much as Paul appeared to be at peace with his past, he was haunted every night by the man whose life he took after surpassing the legal alcohol blood level. During visits into his dreams, I was a recurring passenger in his car and would try to remind him of everything he had done for the sake of his rehabilitation. Yet not once did he turn the steering wheel. Even at the very last second, he drove straight ahead, reliving the worst moment of his life repeatedly.

Obviously, Paul Fletcher's type of closure wouldn't be the same as that of Allie and Edward Martin. Nevertheless, what happened to Beth would likely stay with them one way or another for the rest of their lives. And if that's the case, is there really such thing as closure? For once, and believe me, this was rare, I agreed with Agent Linden. What they needed was justice. At least that was something that could be defined in finite terms.

"Thank you for your time, Mr. Freeman," I said, realizing there was no further need for him. I stood.

Linden stood as well. "We'll see our way out," he said.

Freeman stayed kicked back in his comfortable chair. "Good luck, gentlemen," he said. "It's like my grandfather used to say, just because you disagree with where a man's headed doesn't mean you should wish him well on his journey."

"Thanks," I said.

"Oh, and, by the way, I feel a need to apologize for Candance," he added. "It wasn't easy finding a replacement."

"Replacement?"

"Unfortunately, yes. Our last receptionist, Maggie, quit without notice. It was the damndest thing. One day she was here, and everything seemed fine. The next day, poof, she was gone."

The wheels turned in my head. "Maggie?" I said. "Is that short for Margaret?"

"As a matter of fact, it is. Why do you ask?"

"Just curious. What was her last name?"

"Stevens," he said. "Do you know her?"

Chapter Eight

After getting Margaret Stevens' address from Mr. Freeman, Linden and I arrived at her apartment approximately thirty minutes later. It was in a less affluent part of town, a few miles away from the up-close, majestic views of the Ohio River. We pulled up to the leasing office and got out of the car. An older lady with a sunhat was hunched over a flowerbed pulling weeds in front of the office. We started to walk in but noticed there was no one at the front desk.

"Can I help you?" the older lady said, raising her head and tipping her hat to get a better look at us.

Linden flashed his badge. "I'm Agent Linden of the FBI," he said. "We're looking for Apartment 7C."

She tilted her head in the direction of a series of apartments. "It's over yonder," she said.

"Are you the apartment manager?" Linden inquired

"Yep," she said, stuffing a handful of weeds into a plastic grocery bag. "And apparently the landscaper."

"Do you know Margaret Stevens?" I asked.

"Yeah, I know her," she said and got up to face us. "She in some kind of trouble?"

"No," said Linden. "We just want to talk to her."

"Good luck. I ain't seen her come and go in about a week."

Linden reached into his coat pocket and pulled out a picture. He showed it to the apartment manager. It was an engagement photograph of Beth and Bobby. "Do you recognize this woman?" he asked.

The manager studied the picture closely. "Nope," she said. "Is that the victim?"

"What makes you ask that?" said Linden.

"Well, you boys don't normally go around showing folks pictures of your cousin Susie, now do ya?"

Linden smirked. "What about him?" he asked, pointing to Bobby.

"He looks familiar, but I can't place where I seen him."

"Thank you for your time, ma'am," Linden told her, slipping the photo back into his coat pocket.

We left the manager to her yardwork and made our way over to the unit where Margaret Stevens lived. We climbed the stairs to find her apartment and encountered a man as he was coming down with four different dogs on leashes, all pulling him in different directions. As much as I wanted to see if they were going to overpower him and carry him off like in some slapstick comedy, I let him pass and followed Linden to the door with "7C" on it. Linden knocked on the door.

After a few minutes, a pretty, young woman in a bathrobe opened the door a crack but left the chain in place. "Yes?" she said, appearing as if she hadn't slept in days.

"Are you Margaret Stevens?" Linden asked.

She sighed. "Yes," she said. "What do you want?"

"I'm Agent Linden of the FBI," he said. "This is Max Crawford. We'd like to talk to you."

"I don't want to talk to anybody," she said and shut the door.

"Miss Stevens, we need your help!" Linden raised his voice and spoke to the door. "Do you know Beth Martin?!"

"Just go away!" she said through the door.

"What about Bobby Fugate?! You worked with him at the law firm until you quit! Why *did* you quit, Miss Stevens?!"

"It just wasn't working out, okay?!" she replied and began to sob. "Now please! I haven't been feeling well and want to be left alone!"

Linden turned to me. "Can't you read her mind or something?" he asked expectantly.

"Through the door? Who do you think I am? Superman? I need to see her face, or it won't work."

Frustrated, Linden knocked on the door again. "Miss Stevens?!" he said, but, this time, she didn't answer. "Miss

Stevens?!" he repeated. When there was no response, he stepped away from the door and started down the steps. "Come on, Crawford," he said.

"So, what now?" I asked, following him down the stairs.

"We head back to the hospital and you go into Beth's head again," he said matter-of-factly.

I stopped at the end of the stairs. "But what about her?" I asked, pointing up toward Margaret's apartment. "Are we just going to give up?"

He came to a halt and turned to me. "What do you suggest we do?"

"I don't know," I said. "Can't we stake out the apartment?"

"Stakeout? What do you think this is? Some 1980s drug bust movie? She might not come out at all and we have little time as it is."

"Well, she's got to come out sometime."

"For what?"

"To get groceries."

"She can have those delivered."

"Okay, then what if she needs...I don't know...tampons or something."

"They deliver those too."

"Really?"

"It's the twenty-first century, Crawford, and humanity is lazier than ever. Trust me. There's nothing they won't deliver. Now come on. You've got work to do."

We went back to the hospital and headed straight for Beth's room. I opened the door to find Allie and Edward sitting on either side of the hospital bed. Allie was holding Beth's hand and gently stroking her head. Edward sat and stared at the floor. When I walked in, Allie stood and stepped away from the bed. Edward didn't budge. It was as if he was in a trance, unaffected by everything around him.

"I'm sorry, Mr. Crawford," Allie said, wiping a tear away from her eye. "We don't mean to be in your way."

"You're not in my way, Mrs. Martin," I said. I motioned to the chair. "Please, have a seat. I'm sure Beth would be glad to know you're both here."

Allie sat down and looked at her daughter's face. "They grow up so fast," she said. "Do you have children, Mr. Crawford?"

"I have one," I replied. "Her name's Katie."

"Enjoy every moment," she said. "Because you never know when..." She started to cry.

I grabbed a box of tissues off a nearby counter and handed them to her.

"Thank you," she said, pulling one from the box and dabbing her eyes. "Have you made any progress?" she asked.

"Some," I said, trying to reassure her. "Do you know a woman named Margaret Stevens? She used to work with Mr. Fugate at the law firm."

She shook her head. "No. Does that name mean anything to you, Edward?"

He snapped out of his daze. "Does what mean anything to me?" he said.

"Margaret Stevens," she said the name louder this time, as if her husband's hearing aid was turned down. "Do you recognize the name?"

He shrugged. "I knew a Margaret Ellingsworth back in school. She had a heifer she used to walk to school every day. Drove the teachers crazy."

Allie frowned. "I'm sorry, Mr. Crawford. I don't think we can help you there. Is this Margaret Stevens person somehow involved with what happened to Beth?"

"That's what I'm trying to find out. I do have one other question for you if don't mind."

"Sure," she said.

"Did you ever own a dog?" I asked.

"We've owned a few over the years. Why?"

"Was there one that Beth was particularly fond of named Petey?"

"Yep," Edward chimed in. "Mangy little mutt but Beth loved it like it was one of her dolls."

"Oh, that's right," Allie said, remembering. "Petey. Beth must've been six or seven. What ever happened to that dog?"

"Ran away, I suppose," Edward said listlessly. "They all do eventually."

"There wasn't any kind of...accident you can recall?" I asked cautiously.

"No," Allie said, shaking her head. "Why?"

"Well, Beth, or some part of Beth, seems to think that she killed him."

"Oh, heavens no!" Allie exclaimed. "Beth wouldn't hurt a fly. She must be confused."

I nodded. "That is a good possibility," I explained. "In my line of work, fact and fiction often get mixed up. Memories can get altered because of someone's perception of them. Sometimes they get so muddy, it's hard to tell what actually happened and what the mind created."

Allie reached over and touched Beth's face. "The poor thing," she said. "She must feel so lost in there." She turned toward me and stood again. "Let's go, Edward," she said. "Mr. Crawford needs to get back to work."

Edward started to get up when a young doctor entered the room. "Who are you?" Edward asked.

"This is Doctor Matson, honey," Allie explained. "You met him two days ago."

"Oh, yeah," Edward said.

"I'm sure you two have met so many people here it's hard to keep up," said Doctor Matson. "How are you both doing?"

"Best we can," answered Allie. She motioned to me. "This is Mr. Crawford," she told the doctor. "He's here to help find out what happened to Beth."

Doctor Matson extended his hand. "Nice to meet you, Mr. Crawford," he said.

"You as well," I said, shaking his hand.

"I'm going to take a look at her vitals," he said, getting to business. He walked over and glanced at the monitors attached to Beth. "Everything is about the same as last time."

"Any idea when she might wake up?" asked Allie.

"Mrs. Martin," Doctor Matson spoke gravely. "I don't want to give you false hope. Your daughter has experienced great trauma. Right now, she's holding on with everything she's got."

"She always was a fighter," said Allie.

Doctor Matson nodded. "That's good," he said. "I'm sure

having you here by her side has helped too. Trust me. We'll continue monitoring her and do what we can. But, ultimately, only time will tell."

"Thank you, Doctor," Allie said, her face betraying her attempt at a jovial tone.

"You're welcome," he said. "I'll come by this afternoon and check on her again."

After Doctor Matson left, Allie and Edward both started for the door. I wanted to give them some words of encouragement but couldn't think of any that wouldn't sound forced or belittle what they were experiencing. But then I imagined Katie lying there in Beth's place and nearly choked up at the thought. I would need someone to reassure me if I were in their position.

"I know I haven't gotten any answers," I said to them on their way out. "But I want you to know I'm not going to stop until I do."

"Thank you, Mr. Crawford," said Allie. "You're a good man."

After they left, I walked over to the chair beside Beth and sat down. My phone buzzed and I pulled it out of my pocket. Jessica had texted me asking how it was going. I told her and then asked how Katie had been dealing with her inherited psychic abilities. She replied with a frownie face emoji and said she got into trouble at school again. Only this time it was for cheating in math class. Her teacher confronted her when she saw that she had the same exact answers as the boy next to her. She insisted that she didn't look at this paper, but the teacher didn't believe her. She got detention and later admitted to Jessica that she had read his mind.

I tried to assure her that it was just growing pains. I told her Katie would eventually become more responsible with her powers and that we needed to be patient with her. She replied with three frownie face emojis in a row. She then said she missed me and to come home soon. I promised I'd go home as soon as I could. We exchanged "I Love You's" and I slipped the phone back into my pocket.

I refocused on the task at hand and prepared myself to enter Beth's mind. I settled into my chair, took a few deep breaths, and blocked out the beeping sounds coming from the hospital equipment. Once I was ready, I focused in on her face. I was about to project when something caught me off guard. I looked closer, but it was gone. I tried convincing myself I was imagining things, but, for a split second, I could've sworn she was smiling.

Chapter Nine

Once inside, I was standing in the lobby of Beth's "retirement" hotel. I noticed someone familiar standing at the check-in counter and, upon a closer look, saw that it was Bobby Fugate.

I kept my distance, curious as to what Beth's dream version of her fiancé might do next. After a few moments at the check-in counter, he walked toward one of the hallways of rooms, toting a rolling suitcase behind him. I followed him, discreetly, making sure not to draw attention to myself.

About halfway down the hall, he stopped and took out a key. He opened the door and started to step inside. He glanced back at me and I pretended to dig out a key for one of the other rooms. He went in and closed the door behind him. I approached the room he had entered and saw that the number "6" was on the door. If Beth's number sequence stayed the same that meant "Room 31," which was her room in a previous visit, must be close by.

I went to turn the door handle but noticed that the door was propped open by the metal security bar. I heard low music coming from inside. It was "Let's Get It On" by Marvin Gaye. I cautiously pushed the door open but couldn't see Bobby. I could, however, hear him moaning on the bed. I stepped inside and carefully let the door rest against the metal security bar.

I stealthily crept along the wall and peeked around the corner, ready to make a run for it if necessary.

To my surprise and confusion, Bobby was naked, blindfolded, and lying on the bed. All around him were hundred-dollar bills. He picked up a handful of bills and rubbed them all over his body. As he did this, he rolled around on the bed in ecstasy, groaning louder and louder.

Once he was done with the first bunch of bills, he grabbed more and repeated the process.

Deciding I had seen enough, I tiptoed out of the room and quietly let the door prop up against the metal security bar again.

I walked a little way down the hall and, as expected, found a room with "31" on it. I knocked and, within a few seconds, Beth opened the door. She wore all black, including a small hat with a thin veil that covered her eyes. I heard somber organ music coming from inside the room. Through a crack in the door, I saw a group of people sitting in chairs in front of a closed wooden casket.

She sighed. "I thought you were the priest," she said. "He's running late."

"Priest?" I probed.

"To give the eulogy, of course," she said as if I had asked her if the sky was blue. "You're Mr. Crawford. Aren't you?"

"Yes," I said, for a second forgetting I was wearing my normal face and not Bobby's.

"Are you coming in or not?" she asked.

I hesitantly stepped inside, and she closed the door behind us. Among the group of people near the cast was an older woman dressed in the same black outfit as Beth. She started sniffling and then suddenly broke out into full-blown wailing. She got up from her seat and came over to us. Beth wrapped her arms around her and patted her back to console her. The woman buried her face into a tissue and blew her nose in an almost comical fashion.

"There, there," Beth said. "It's okay."

The woman finally slowed down to a more controlled sob and released herself from Beth's embrace. "Thank you," she said, blotting her eyes with the tissue. She looked at me and forced a smile. "How did you know the deceased?" she asked.

"Me?" I said, trying to stall for an answer. Having no idea who the hell was in the casket, I chose a more generalist approach. "We, uh, were neighbors at one point."

The woman began to speak but burst into tears again. "I'm

sorry for your loss!" she eventually said and then wept all the
way back to her seat.

Beth turned to me and motioned expectantly toward the
casket. "Well?"

"Well what?" I said.

"Don't you want to say your goodbyes?" she asked
impatiently.

"Of course," I answered, continuing to play along. "I'll, uh,
do that right now."

"You'll need to lift the lid," she said matter-of-factly. "We
had it open earlier but it got to be too much for everyone to
bear."

I nodded. "That's understandable," I said, seriously regret-
ting having come into the room in the first place.

I moved toward the coffin with trepidation. I halfway
expected to open it and have Beth's demon counterpart leap out
and try to choke me to death again. I stopped at the casket and
turned to look at her. She repetitively rolled her hand in a circle
as if to say, "hurry it up." The others watched me with bated
breath. I faced the coffin and braced myself. I slipped my fingers
underneath the wood and slowly lifted the lid.

When I saw what was inside, I had to do a double take.
At first, I thought it was a large, hairy raisin. But, upon closer
inspection, I realized it was a cocoon. It was brown and bumpy,
covered in a layer of translucent slime. It was about six feet by
three feet and fit the dimension of the casket perfectly. Just
when I thought things couldn't get stranger, it started to pulsate
rhythmically as if there was a heart beating inside.

The older woman who'd had an emotional outburst moments
earlier rose from her seat, came over, and stood beside me. She
was now eerily tranquil and collected. "It's beautiful, isn't it?"
she said calmly.

"What's in there?" I asked.

"Everything," she replied. "The Alpha and the Omega.
Heaven and Earth. It's where I end, and you begin."

"So, it's alive?"

"It is in the process of becoming."

"Then why do we have to say 'goodbye'?"

"So, we can say 'hello,'" answered Beth as she joined us. "But we can't do that until the godforsaken priest gets here." She walked away from the casket and sat down on one of the empty chairs. "I wish I knew what was taking him so long."

"So, after the priest says a few words," I hypothesized. "This…" I pointed to the cocoon. "…Being will transition to its next state?"

"You're a regular Sherlock Holmes," said Beth.

A sudden uneasiness came over me. The doctor I had met only moments earlier in Beth's hospital room said she was holding on with everything she's got. What he didn't mention was that, on some level, she might be getting tired of holding on. If somehow the cocoon was a representation of her and its "transitioning" reflected her own desire to let go of the earthly realm, I needed to do everything possible to keep it from happening.

"Why don't I go look for the priest?" I suggested. "He probably just got lost trying to find your room."

She shrugged. "Whatever speeds this along," she said nonchalantly.

"And to be clear," I continued. "Your name is still…"

"Margaret Stevens," she said with a look like I had lost my mind. "Maybe I should be the one to go look for the priest."

"No," I insisted. "You stay here. I'll be right back."

"Fine," she said, crossing her arms like a defiant teenager. "But hurry it up, will ya? We don't have all day."

I nodded and stepped outside into the hallway. Complicating matters even further was the fact that Beth's emotional state was affecting her personality. Not only was she still "Margaret Stevens" but she was also becoming more apathetic. If being Margaret was somehow helping her let go, I needed to hurry or else risk the possibility of her real self-disappearing completely.

I moved down the hall back in the direction of the main lobby area. Once I was there, I noticed there were more people than normal. There were at least a dozen standing in line at the check-in counter. I rushed to the front of the queue but was quickly pushed aside by a hairy, robust man wearing a loose-fitting tank top that said, "Give me a beer and I'll see the light," and cut-off blue jeans shorts that left little to the imagination.

"Hey!" he said in an almost comical husky voice. "Get to the back of the line, buddy!"

"I'm sorry," I said, looking at the man behind the counter. "It's an emergency. I was wondering if you'd seen a priest."

"Sir, please go to the back of the line," said the man. "These people have been waiting their whole lives to check in. If I were to answer your question it would be a disservice to each and every one of them."

"Really?" I said. "In all the time it took you to say all of that you could've just answered my question."

"Sir, don't make me alert security," he said, motioning to the half-human, half-alien "security guards," or as Beth referred to them, Grilax and Grulax, standing near the front entrance.

"Alright," I said, wanting to avoid getting thrown out again. "I'll just find him myself."

I turned away from the counter to see that the lobby was now full of people. Hundreds of men and women of all ages packed the room to the point where there was no room to move around. Every one of them was gravitating toward the check-in counter. I began to feel claustrophobic as they surrounded me at all sides. Complicating matters even further, I noticed a man dressed as a priest making his way toward the hallway leading to Beth's room.

I tried pushing my way through the crowd, but it was no use. They were too strong a barrier. Then I remembered I wasn't in the real world. I willed myself to levitate eight feet off the ground and float over their heads toward the priest. Since they were so focused on checking in, none of them even paid any attention to the fact I was hovering above them like some strange, other-worldly wizard. Once I was clear of the crowd, I landed safely at the end of the hallway.

The priest was already halfway down the corridor, so I ran after him. Right as he casually made it to Beth's door, I caught up with him. He reached out to knock but I tackled him to the ground before he had the chance. He started to yell out for help, but I quickly covered his mouth and pinned him to the floor. He struggled to break free, but I held him down, all the while realizing how ridiculous such a thing would've appeared outside of a dream.

"You can go now," I told him. "Your services are not needed at this time."

He stopped resisting and looked at me curiously. Though his arms were restrained, his hands were free. He lifted a finger and pointed to Beth's door. I shook my head. Next, he seemed confused. I removed my hand from his mouth, ready to cover it again if he started to scream.

"Are you sure?" he said. "I feel like I should go in there."

"I'm positive," I said. "It's not the right time."

He nodded. Before I could get up and help him to his feet, he began to shake beneath me. All of a sudden, miniscule pieces of him began to flake off from his body and float down the hall. His head was the last to go. He smiled at me as his face slowly dissolved into tiny particles that drifted away to join the others. Since there was nothing left to hold down, I stood up to watch as thousands of specks formed a large circle at the end of the hall, swirled around for a moment, and then disappeared completely.

Chapter Ten

I went to Beth's door and knocked. No one answered. After another attempt, I walked further down the hall until the sequence of room numbers started over again. Thinking perhaps following them in order might shed some light on the case, I tapped on the door with a "2" on it and waited. Right as I was about to move on to the room with the "6" on it, and previously the one where Beth's mental version of Bobby Fugate made strange and disturbing love to hundred-dollar bills, someone cracked open the door. Half-glad I didn't have to witness imaginary Bobby's cash-sex fest again and half-curious, I peeked in closer to see the young man from earlier with the faux hawk and Ramones t-shirt staring back at me.

"What do you want?" he asked, obviously hiding something.

"I'm looking for Beth," I said.

"You her uncle or something?" he inquired, eyeing me suspiciously.

"No."

"You a cop?" he continued his interrogation.

"No," I replied.

"You sure? 'Cause if you are, you gotta tell me. I know all about entrapment."

"I'm sure you do but you can put your guilty conscience at ease," I assured him. "I'm not a cop."

"Wait a second then," he said and shut the door in my face.

A minute or so later, the door opened again. Teenage Beth peeked through the crack. Her hair was disheveled, and her eyes were bloodshot. "What do you want?" she asked.

"I just want to talk to you," I said.

She looked me up and down then wiped her nose with her shirt sleeve. "You got any weed?" she asked.

"Oh, yes," I said and willed a pound bag of make-believe marijuana to appear in my hands. "Really good shit."

Her eyes lit up and she quickly opened the door. "Su casa es mi casa," she said eagerly and motioned for me to enter.

"I think you have that backward."

"What backward?"

"Never mind," I said and stepped inside with the imaginary pot.

The room was more of a teenager's bedroom than a hotel room. There were posters of musicians on the wall that I'd never heard of, along with a few I had. The most familiar was of Jim Morrison, lead singer of The Doors and well before Beth's time yet timeless all the same.

There was also a single mattress with no sheets on the floor, making it appear as if Teenage Beth and her male companion were squatting rather than staying officially.

All of this was seen through a thin haze that filled the room. There were no overhead lights, only a red lamp in the corner that gave the room an almost stereotypical drug den vibe.

The faux hawk fellow was taking a hit from a one-foot-tall hookah on a lopsided table with a missing leg and a pile of phone books in its place. Beth sat next to him, took the vinyl hose attached to the hookah from him and inhaled through the wooden mouthpiece. She exhaled and looked at me impatiently, an age-defying glare like the one she gave me only moments earlier in her adult form.

"What are you waiting for?" she said impudently. "Let's fire it up."

I sat down on the floor across from them and laid the pretend pound bag on the table.

Beth scooped it up and opened it. She smelled inside the bag and smiled. She handed it to her companion, who also took a whiff and gave me an approving nod. What they didn't know was that it wasn't real and didn't smell like anything at all. Placebos can be a powerful tool, even in the recesses of someone's mind.

Beth's companion proceeded to roll an imaginary joint. "What's your name, man?" he asked.

"I'm Max," I said. "What's yours?"

"Charlie," he said.

"Charlie's in a band," said Beth.

"I play guitar," said Charlie. "You ever heard of 'Bunny Shot Jesus Dream'?"

"I can't say I have," I said.

"Well, we ain't big yet but we will be one day," he said.

I would later discover that Charlie had been Beth's high school boyfriend. According to her mother, she went through quite the rebellious phase before becoming a responsible adult. Charlie, on the other hand, didn't turn out so well. A few years after high school, he was on his way to play in a "Battle of the Bands" festival when his inebriated driver/bass player friend ran into a semi head-on and killed everyone except the drummer.

Charlie finished rolling the joint and lit it. He took a hit. "Not bad," he said, holding in the smoke. "Where'd you get this stuff?"

"To be honest with you, it just materialized in my hands," I explained.

He laughed and coughed up the smoke. "You're crazy, man."

"Give it here," Beth said, grabbing the joint from him. She motioned to me. "I wanna get as high as he is." She pressed it to her lips and inhaled. She then held it out for me to take.

"No, thanks," I said.

"What do you mean 'no thanks'?" asked Charlie. "I thought you said you weren't a cop."

Beth exhaled. "Take it or get the hell out of here," she said. "Charlie's already been to juvie twice. I'm not gonna let it happen again."

Not wanting to forfeit an opportunity to connect with another side of Beth, I accepted the dream joint from her. I had only tried marijuana once. An ex-girlfriend in college used it regularly and decided to initiate me at a 20,000-capacity outdoor music festival. Once it kicked in, the sounds, people, and overall environment seemed to engulf me. Feelings of paranoia and claustrophobia set in, causing a panic that forced me to leave.

My ex-girlfriend later found me in the parking lot rambling to an attendant about the benefits of transcendental meditation.

I took a puff and then handed it to Charlie. After a few seconds, something strange happened. I don't know if it was Beth's unconscious mind altering my perception or my own experience influencing the situation, but I started to feel high. Charlie inhaled, exhaled, and then lay back on the floor and shut his eyes. Beth took the joint out of his hand and helped herself to more. She looked at me closely.

"I know what you are," she said.

"What?" I asked, trying to conceal the fact the room was spinning a bit.

"You're a demon," she said. "I knew it the moment you walked in here." She handed me the joint. "It's okay. You can't help what you are."

"I'm not a demon," I said, giggling involuntarily. "I'm a friend."

"All demons say that," she said. She pointed to the joint. "Puff and pass, man."

"Sorry," I said, taking another imaginary hit. I handed it back to her. "What makes you think I'm a demon?"

She laughed. "Your horns," she said, motioning to my forehead.

I felt around on top of my head and discovered that I did, in fact, have horns protruding out of it. "What the hell?" I said.

"Told you so," she said in a childish voice then partook some more. "You got a tail too."

I looked behind me and saw a red and scaly, devil-like tail sticking out of my backside.

Realizing Beth was projecting characteristics on to me, I didn't panic. I stayed calm, hoping to present myself as normal despite the fact I was transforming into a half-Satan, half-human hybrid. Beth seemed to be enjoying it. She moved closer to me, reached out, and laid her hand on the appendage. To my surprise, the tail recoiled from her and formed a resting spiral behind me.

"Don't be so touchy," she said. "I only wanted to feel it."

"Evidently it has a mind of its own," I said. "So, what makes me a demon exactly? Do you think I'm evil?"

"You're neither good nor evil," she explained. "You are what you are. People might make you out to be evil, but that's just their conditioning. You know, years of being told you're bad and should be avoided at all costs. The truth is you're no better or worse than the rest of us. Just different."

"I see. So, are there other demons in your life?"

"That's kind of a personal question, Max," she replied. "Seeing as we only met a little while ago, I'm not sure I'm comfortable answering it."

"I understand," I said, intending to probe cautiously. "Do you mind if I ask you another question then?"

"Go right ahead," she answered.

"If I'm a demon, what are you?"

She looked at me seriously for a second and then smiled. Big, fluffy white wings sprouted from her shoulder blades, flapped momentarily, and then became still. "You tell me," she said grinning.

"Nice wings," I said. "Did you earn those?"

"Very funny," she said. "Who are you really? You seem familiar to me. Were you my ninth-grade algebra teacher?"

"No."

"Then where do I know you from?"

"Maybe another time in your life? Perhaps when you were younger...or older?"

"Older?" she laughed. "How would that be possible?"

"You'd be surprised. By the way, how do your parents feel about you and Charlie hanging out?"

"Oh, Jesus. You were my school counselor."

"No. Just curious."

"My dad's oblivious and my mom thinks I'm hanging out with a girlfriend. Charlie doesn't fit in with their boring farming-life mentality, so they'd probably freak out."

"So, they'd worry about you?"

"Definitely. They're always overreacting."

"Or they want you to be safe. It's a crazy world out there. Just the other day, a woman was nearly beaten to death on her way home from her parents' house. Now she's in a coma."

Her wings began to shrink. "That's awful," she said.

"Yeah. I want to help her, but I don't know how. I have very few clues and, to be honest, feel like I'm chasing my tail. What do you think I should do, Beth?"

Her wings disappeared into her shoulder blades and she rubbed her forehead. "I think that stuff's getting to my head," she said. "I don't feel so good."

I noticed that my horns and tail had vanished as well. "Maybe you should lie down so we can talk some more," I suggested, hoping I was reaching a possible breakthrough.

She suddenly stood up and started hyperventilating. "I don't want to talk anymore!" she screamed, breathing heavily.

Once again, before my eyes, Beth transformed into the crimson creature with the pitch-black eyes and sharp, pointy teeth. After shedding her teenage body, it let out a shriek that startled Charlie out of his pot-induced snooze. Charlie jumped up and looked at the beast in shock. He quickly grabbed the hookah off the table. He swung it at the creature, but it swiped it out of his hand and, with one speedy lunge, bit off his head. Blood spewed from Charlie's neck, but it wasn't just red. It was all the colors of the rainbow, shooting out of his headless body like some freaky children's playground fountain. He fell to the floor and didn't move.

Before I could beat myself up for pushing Teenage Beth too hard and too soon, the creature barreled toward me. I jumped out of the way and it ran into a dresser, knocking off a lamp that came crashing to the floor. I ran for the door, but it was right behind me. It grabbed me and sunk its teeth into my shoulder. I let out a yelp, mainly out of surprise since I didn't actually feel anything. I kicked the creature in the stomach, sending it flying backward and causing it to topple over onto its backside.

While it was on the ground, I hurriedly opened the door. Right as I was about to step outside, it got up and ran straight at me, squealing at the top of its lungs. I shut the door right before it pounced on me. I heard it banging madly on the walls and shrieking loudly inside the room. The other nearby rooms, however, were completely quiet, seemingly undisturbed by the madness.

Chapter Eleven

I was moving toward "Room 7" to see if Little Beth was there when the hallway started to vibrate. I braced myself against the wall, wondering if Beth was having some sort of disturbance in her brain. The vibrating stopped only to begin again seconds later. Pieces of the ceiling broke off and fell to the floor. I decided that, if something was happening, it was best for me to exit and let a nurse know. I withdrew from her mind and back into the hospital room. As it turned out, it was my cell phone buzzing in my pants pocket. I took it out and saw Katie's picture on the screen.

"Katie?" I answered.

"Dad," she said through the line, her voice shaking. "I'm not doing so good."

"What is it, peanut?" I asked.

"The voices," she answered. "I can't make them stop."

I got up from my chair and walked over to the window. "Yes, you can, sweetheart," I told her. "And they're not voices, remember? They're other people's thoughts and you can shut them out. Where are you right now?"

"I'm in my room. I told the school nurse I was having my period and she let me come home."

"That's more information than I needed but okay," I said, trying to lighten the situation.

"You're not helping!" She giggled nervously. "What do I do?"

"First of all, only look directly at someone if necessary and, when you do, make sure it's only for as long as he or she is speaking. Once they stop, look away."

"For how long?"

"Until either you or they start speaking again."

"I'm so screwed."

Linden entered the room and I held my finger up to signal "just a minute." "Look," I said to Katie. "I know it's overwhelming right now, but it'll get better, I promise. Just practice what I told you. I gotta go but I'll call you later. I love you, peanut."

"I love you, too," she said. "Call me back as soon as you can."

"I will," I said. "Bye, sweetheart."

I ended the call and turned to face Linden. "My daughter," I told him. "She plays volleyball at her school and needed a pep talk."

Linden was the last person I would tell about Katie's developing psychic abilities. First of all, it's up to Katie who she shares it with and, secondly, there was no way I'd let her get put on a government list of potential specialists so they could recruit her for some future assignment. I didn't want her to have to experience the horrors I had and, frankly, hoped to protect her from them as long as I could.

"Must be tough being a dad," he said.

"It can be," I said. "You ever thought about having kids, Agent Linden?"

"Hell, no," he replied. "After the shit I've seen, not a chance. Speaking of which, Margaret Stevens was found dead in her apartment an hour ago."

"Damn. Suicide?"

"It appears that way, but we won't know for certain until forensics gets done with the scene. Maintenance discovered her in the bathtub with her wrists slit. I thought it might be good for us to go and look. Maybe something in her apartment could give us a clue as to why she did it or what it has to do with Beth."

On the way to Margaret Stevens' apartment, I perused a file on her that Linden had brought along. She had a long history of depression, beginning in high school when she spent a week in a treatment facility after trying to overdose on pain pills. She later regularly saw a psychiatrist who prescribed various medications until one finally did the trick. She went without incident for several years but then, shortly after Beth was attacked, returned to see the psychiatrist. Evidently, this time it didn't go as well.

In addition to depression, Margaret had also been treated for drug and alcohol abuse.

She had been arrested on one occasion for a DWI, received counseling, and, following a probationary period had no subsequent run-ins with the law. According to her employers, she was a model employee during her short time working at the Law Offices of Baxter, Freeman, and Lester. So much so that it came as a complete shock to them when she quit abruptly and without explanation.

"You don't think it was our visit that finally pushed her over the edge, do you?" I asked

Linden as we approached her apartment building.

He shrugged. "Maybe," he answered nonchalantly. "But then it's possible she'd been planning it all along and was going to do it either way. When I first started out with the bureau, we investigated a man accused of embezzling money from a very high-profile corporation. He swore up and down that he didn't do it. Right as we were getting close to the truth, he jumped off a thirty-story building. A few days later, we discovered that it was his secretary that had stolen the money. He was completely innocent."

"Then why did he kill himself?" I asked.

"Who the hell knows?" he replied. "Did he think he was going to be found guilty? Was he hiding something even worse? Or was he just a nut job that slipped through the cracks when the school counselor passed out pamphlets about the importance of expressing your feelings? My point is you can drive yourself crazy wondering why but, ultimately, it doesn't make any difference. A person ended his life and there's nothing you can do to bring him back."

"I never realized there were so many layers to you, Linden," I jested. "I always figured you for a two-dimensional type."

"I'm practical," he said as he parked in the same spot in front of the leasing office he did the last time. "Now let's go see the dead girl's apartment."

A small crowd gathered near the stairwell leading to Margaret's residence. We got out of the car and moved toward them. Among the spectators were the apartment manager and a tanned maintenance man with three-day stubble and a shell-shocked look on his face. We made our way to the front of the mob and the apartment manager. She was just as excited to see us as she was on our first visit.

"Oh, it's you two," she said. "I hope you're not back for more questions. Maggie's—"

"We know," Linden interrupted her. "Are you the one that found her?" he addressed the maintenance man.

"Yeah," he said with a distance gaze in his eyes. "I was just going to check the stove. Ms. Stevens had called about it goin' out yesterday, but I couldn't get to it till today. I can't help but think this wouldn't have happened if I'd gone when she first reached out to me."

"Oh, Glen," the apartment manager said with a deadpan tone. "You're not Jesus. How could you have known she was going to kill herself?"

As tempted as I was to inquire about the apartment manager's apparent belief that Christ had psychic powers, I stayed focused on the matter at hand. "What happened right before you found her?" I asked Glen.

"Well," he continued. "I let myself in with the master key. I called out to Ms. Stevens, but she didn't answer. I was in the hallway when I noticed blood coming out from under the bathroom door. I went in to see if everything was alright and there she was, all bled out. Was she sufferin' from depression? 'Cause I got this cousin that—"

"Thank you for your time," Linden cut him off. "I imagine this experience has been very traumatic for you. We have counselors available if you need to speak to someone." He turned to me. "Come on, Crawford."

I followed Linden through the front of the crowd and up the stairs. One man peeked his head out of his door but quickly shut it when he saw us. When we reached Margaret's apartment, there was a police officer standing in the entryway. Linden flashed his FBI badge and the officer nodded and stepped aside.

Upon entering, I noticed the kitchen had been unattended to for quite some time. A pile of dirty dishes in the sink had attracted flies and a nearby trashcan overflowed onto the floor.

We moved past the living room area, which was equally unkept, and made our way into the hallway by the bathroom. There was a forensic specialist inside taking pictures. Through the open doorway, I saw Margaret's arm draped over the side of the bathtub. Linden pushed the door open and there she was, naked and still in the water. I felt like she was being intruded upon the way the burly man with the camera was snapping pictures of her exposed like that. Then I reminded myself that it didn't bother her. In fact, nothing would ever bother her again.

"Any chance you can get some kind of reading?" Linden asked.

"Seriously?" I replied. "What do you think I am? Some kind of medium?"

"I don't know," he said. "I thought maybe there was something still lingering."

"Nope," I said. "When she goes, it goes."

Linden frowned and then turned to the specialist. "Anything out of the ordinary?" he asked him.

"Not really," the man replied as he took another picture. "I'm almost done here. Once you guys are through poking around, I'll give the all clear for the coroner to wheel her out."

Linden nodded and walked past me to the bedroom. The door was wide open. He stepped inside and started looking around. I cautiously entered and stood near the unmade bed. Linden opened the closet door and riffled through some of her clothes, yet another act that irrationally seemed like an invasion of privacy. Her wardrobe consisted of a few nice dresses, probably used for work, and some more casual wear. There was one t-shirt with an image of the Arc de Triomphe at the Champs-Elysees in Paris.

I suddenly got a chill as I imagined Jessica digging through her closet at home for a kid-friendly outfit to wear. As a kindergarten teacher, she had to keep it simple and avoid clothes that couldn't withstand the occasional splash of paint or student that had a passion for taking a pair of scissors to anything that stood in his way. Linden closed the closet and the vision of Jessica vanished, snapping me back to reality.

"Why don't you check that dresser over there?" he suggested, motioning to a small vanity in the corner. "I'll take a look under the bed."

As Linden leaned down and glanced under the bed as if there might be a monster lurking underneath, I went over to the vanity and found a few jewelry cases and makeup kits. I opened one of the cases and uncovered a couple necklaces, several earring sets, bracelets, and a high school ring. I pulled out one of the drawers and stumbled upon some useless knickknacks but didn't see anything that particularly stood out to me.

"There's nothing here," Linden said as he rose to his feet. "Let's get back to the hospital while there's still time."

Right as I was about to concur and shut the drawer, I spotted a photograph under a stack of old candy wrappers. I picked it up and examined it closely. In what appeared to be a picture taken around Christmas time, Beth was standing in front of a tree. To her right was Oscar Freeman and two men in suits who, given their older ages, I assumed were his law partners, Baxter and Lester. To her left was another man in a suit and, based on his build, I figured it must've been Bobby Fugate. Honestly, it was hard to tell because his head had been meticulously cut out of the picture.

Chapter Twelve

Hoping to catch Fugate at work, Linden and I returned to the Law Offices of Baxter, Freeman, and Lester. When we arrived, Candace, the secretary, was once again on her cell phone, texting away as if her life depended on it. Not surprisingly, she ignored us just like the last time. Linden walked up to her desk and put his hand in front of the screen. She looked at him as if he had snatched her newborn baby out of her hands and thrown it against the wall.

"That was rude," she said, pulling the phone away from Linden.

"Not as rude as failing to acknowledge a visitor," he said. "Especially when it's your job."

"Fine," she huffed and set down the phone. "How can I help you?"

"We need to talk to Bobby Fugate," I said.

"He's not here," she said.

"When will he be back?" Linden asked.

"I have no idea," she said. "He called in sick this morning."

"Hello, gentlemen," a familiar voice spoke behind us.

I turned to see Oscar Freeman standing a few feet away from the desk. "Mr. Freeman," I said.

"Mr. Crawford," he greeted me and then addressed Linden. "Agent Linden. Perhaps we could talk more privately again."

"Of course," Linden answered. "Where are your partners?"

"They're at the courthouse," he replied then motioned toward the hallway. "Please."

We followed him back to the conference room with the mahogany table in the center.

He motioned for us to sit and then took his seat at the head of the table. Once we were all settled, he took a deep breath and paused for a moment. I read his mind to discover that he already knew about Margaret's suicide and was carefully choosing his words before he addressed it.

"I'm sure you fellows heard about Maggie," he finally said. "I couldn't believe it when I got the news. She was a wonderful person and an excellent employee."

"Yeah," Linden chimed in. "We got that part. But what was her relationship with Bobby Fugate?"

"Relationship?" he asked. "They were co-workers."

"Did they spend time together outside the office?" I inquired.

"Not that I'm aware of," he answered.

I checked his thoughts again. He was either telling the truth or doing a great job hiding it from me. And then, from somewhere in his mind, a memory arose. He came into the office one day to find Bobby standing at the front desk and laughing with Margaret. As soon as they saw him, they quickly went back to business as if they had suddenly been caught in the middle of something.

"What about in the office?" I asked, wanting to take advantage of his mental digression.

"I'm sure I don't know what you mean," he said, trying to put the recollection out of his head.

"I think you do," I persisted. "Were they ever…inappropriate with each other at work?"

"God no! They were always—"

"Excellent employees?" I finished his sentence.

"Yes," he said. "Absolutely."

"Is it possible that something else was going on?" I continued. "Something you turned a blind eye to but knew was happening all along?"

"Now you look here," he became defensive. "This is a *professional* establishment. I—"

"Save the speech, Mr. Freeman," Linden interrupted. "A girl is dead, and another is in a coma. Professionalism isn't going to help either of them. If you know of anything that might help us figure this thing out, now is the time to clear your conscience."

"Alright," he said after a long pause. He leaned back in this chair and appeared defeated.

"There were a few times when things between them seemed a little odd."

"Could you be more specific please?" I asked.

"Sometimes I'd find them whispering to each other and, when they saw me, they'd stop."

"Whispering about what?" Linden inquired.

"How should I know?!" Freeman threw his hands in the air. "They were whispering! I couldn't hear!"

"Did Margaret ever meet Beth?" I asked.

"Let me think," he said and pondered on it. "There was this one office party. Family members were invited. I seem to remember Bobby introducing them to each other."

"How did that go?" asked Linden.

"Agent Linden, in my line of work, people meet each other every day. I can't recall the specific details of one particular encounter."

He was lying. The night in question appeared vividly at the forefront of his mind. I let him and Linden go back forth while pieces of the evening unfolded before me like a badly edited movie. It began with Freeman and his partners in the same conference room where we were sitting. They were reminiscing about some case they had recently won and filling their cups from a spiked punchbowl in the middle of the mahogany table. Their wives stood nearby, also drinking and having their own conversation about friends of theirs that weren't in the room. They were all sipping and laughing when Beth and Bobby walked in to the room.

After a few choppy greetings, Bobby joined the men and Beth sat down at the table by herself. He offered her a drink, but she declined. The partners' wives tried to involve her in their banter. She went along with it but, ultimately, seemed to feel awkward being there. The scene then cut to Margaret's arrival. At that point, Bobby had become quite inebriated. Beth watched as he hugged Margaret more closely than fellow employees normally would.

"Let me get you a drink," Bobby told Margaret. He noticed

Beth as if he'd forgotten she was there. "Oh, and this is my fiancée, Beth."

"Nice to meet you," Margaret said and extended her hand.

Beth shook it hesitantly. "Nice to meet you, too," she said.

The scene then abruptly switched to later in the evening.
Beth was still sitting in the same spot, but Bobby and Margaret
were noticeably absent. Freeman walked over to Beth and
tried talking to her, but she didn't acknowledge him. From her
crossed arms and icy glare, it was obvious that she was angry.
Freeman shrugged and went back to the others. A few seconds
later, Bobby and Margaret entered the room laughing.

Beth rose to her feet. "Where were you?" she asked.

"What's the big deal?" slurred Bobby. "Maggie was just
showing me her new car."

"I'm ready to go now," Beth said, trying to stay calm.

"But we just got here," he said.

"I want to go home!" she raised her voice, causing everyone to stop mid-conversation and turn to look at her. "Please,"
she added more quietly, as if doing so would cause the sudden
attention to her to go away.

"Fine," Bobby said and then stormed drunkenly out of the
room.

"I'm sorry," Beth told everyone and then left as well.

Back in the conference room and out of Freeman's head,
Linden was still pushing for more information. "Surely there's
another time you can remember," he said to Freeman. "Did they
ever go on extended lunch dates?"

"That'll do," I said before he could answer. I stood up to
leave. "You've been very helpful, Mr. Freeman."

"You're...welcome?" Freeman said with a bewildered look
on his face.

Once outside, Linden walked beside me as we approached
the car. "Did you see something?" he asked.

"Yep."

"Should we talk to Lester and Baxter?"

"Probably be a waste of time. I doubt they know any more
than Freeman. The only person I want to talk to right now is
Bobby Fugate."

We hopped in the car and headed uptown to Fugate's apartment. Quite the upgrade from Margaret's complex, a gate separated the residents from the outside world. An attendant waved us in after seeing Linden's badge and we parked near the unit where Fugate lived. We got out of the car and went straight to his door on the second floor. I pressed the buzzer and waited. No response. I hit it a second time.

"It's like I told you," said Linden. "He doesn't have to speak to us."

"Yes?" a voice finally came through the speaker.

"Mr. Fugate, it's Max Crawford and Agent Linden of the FBI," I spoke into the microphone. "We need to talk to you."

"Why don't you two just go away?" he said, sounding slightly broken. "Haven't you done enough already?"

"Actually, we're just getting started," said Linden. "What was your relationship with Margaret Stevens?"

There was a long pause. "I'm not going to talk about Maggie," he finally said.

"What about Beth then?" I added. "She's not in a good place."

"No, shit," he said.

"It's more than you realize," I continued. "She believes she's Margaret."

"What the hell are you talking about?" he said.

"She thinks she's Margaret," I reiterated. "She doesn't seem to remember who she really is."

"She's in a coma, asshole," he said. "How could she think she's somebody else?"

"That's what we're trying to figure out," I said. "We thought maybe you could shed some light on the situation."

"Now you listen here," he said, his voice becoming threatening. "I don't know what mind games you two are trying to play, but it's really starting to piss me off! If you had any decency, you'd leave me and my fiancée alone! Do not come here again!"

After that, the speaker went silent. Linden and I went back to the car. We were on our way to the hospital when the forensic specialist at Margaret's apartment called Linden.

Evidently, he had discovered Margaret's cell phone hidden under a couch in the living room not long after we left. He told

Linden he'd hold on to it, so we could check it before he bagged it. We passed the exit for the hospital and headed straight for Margaret's apartment.

When we got there, the crowd that gathered earlier had disappeared. Even the manager and Glen, the maintenance man that discovered Margaret, were gone. We climbed the stairs and went inside. Margaret's body had been taken away, but her blood was still on the bathroom floor.

We found the forensic specialist waiting for us in the living room. He handed the phone to Linden.

"You'll need to charge it," he said. "It's been dead for a while."

Linden plugged it in a wall outlet and, once it was on, bypassed the password screen. I stood beside him as he scrolled through her phone records. If there had been any calls between her and Bobby, they had been deleted. He then checked voicemail. Also empty. It wasn't until he clicked on the text message application that he found something. There had been an exchange between Bobby and Margaret the night before.

Maggie: I can't keep doing this, Bobby.

Bobby: Keep doing what? You need to calm down.

Maggie: How can I calm down?! Beth's in a coma! The FBI came by to see me! I can't understand how you're calm!

Bobby: Maggie, I promise you. It's going to be okay.

Maggie: It's not going to be okay, Bobby! They're going to find out and, when they do, I'm not going to be around!

Bobby: What do you mean by that?

Bobby: Maggie, are you still there?

Bobby: Look, I'll call you in the morning, okay? Just stay put like we talked about. We'll figure it out.

There were no texts before that, but Margaret could've deleted those as well. Just as Linden appeared as if he was ready to storm into Fugate's apartment and arrest him on the spot, a plan came to mind. I took the phone from him and went into Margaret's photo application. I looked through several pictures of her and watched a couple videos to get a good grasp on her voice patterns and mannerisms. There was one that I viewed three times because it had close-ups of her sitting on the beach and talking to someone off-screen about how much she loved it. I studied every little characteristic and, within a few minutes, had what I needed.

Chapter Thirteen

Back at the hospital, I headed straight for Beth's room. Margaret was fresh in my mind and I needed to hurry or else chance a lack of authenticity. I entered the room and sat down across from Beth. I focused on her face and, after a couple of seconds, projected into her head. I materialized in the familiar hallway and moved toward "Room 31." I reached the door and started to transform into Margaret. Before I could make the change, however, a door opened behind me.

"It's you!" said the young voice. "Please, help me!"

I turned to see Little Beth standing in front of "Room 7." "What's wrong?" I asked.

"Our house is on fire!" she cried. "Please, hurry!"

I moved away from "Room 31," trying to retain Margaret's personality in my memory. I followed Little Beth into "Room 7." Crossing the threshold transported us to her family's farmhouse. Only, instead of the picturesque view of her childhood home and the open landscape on either side, the whole place was in flames. I heard screams coming from inside. Little Beth looked at me pleadingly.

"My mommy and daddy are in there!" she screamed. "Please do something!"

Thinking quickly, I willed a fire truck to appear beside us. I grabbed hold of the hose and aimed it at the burning house. A powerful spray of water shot out of the hose. I went from left to right, extinguishing the fire in pieces. Eventually the flames disappeared, leaving a charcoaled hull before us. Little Beth walked toward it, her hands shaking as she approached the empty shell. She was about to climb what was left of the stairs leading to the front porch when they collapsed at her feet.

"I wouldn't go any further!" I warned her.

"But my parents are in there!" she said, tears rolling down her cheeks. "I have to save them!"

Not wanting to tell her that, if her parents were in the house, there was nothing she could do to help them, I moved closer and took her by the hand. I led her to the edge of the porch and lifted her up onto it. I hoisted myself up onto the porch and stood with her near the front door to the house, which now hung off its hinges. As painful as it was for me to contemplate what we might find inside and how it would affect her, I couldn't risk standing in the way of where her mind needed to go.

I pushed the broken front door to the side, and it fell onto the porch with a smack. The thin wooden boards beneath my feet reverberated hollowly and forebodingly. I half-expected to break through them and drop to the earth below, the same sacred ground where we had found their ill-fated dog Petey on the other side of the house. I promptly followed Little Beth inside, escaping a possible pitfall for the time being.

We passed through the living room, all the furniture blackened and no longer emitting the feel of hearth and home, and moved down a creaky hallway. Little Beth peeked through a door into a small bedroom. There was a tiny bed in the corner that had been reduced to ashes and a doll with soot across its face in the middle of the floor. Little Beth walked over to the plaything and picked it up carefully. She held it up for me to see.

"This is Dolly," she said hopefully. "She survived. Maybe my parents did too."

She took Dolly with her out of the room and into the hallway. She led me to a closed door at the end of the corridor. I smelled burned flesh on the other side. Little Beth went to open the door, but I stood in her way. Although entering the room potentially meant a step closer to getting answers, I, nevertheless, became protective of Beth in her childlike state. I crouched down on one knee and met her at eye level.

"Why don't I go first?" I suggested. "Then I can tell you what's in there before you see it."

She nodded. I braced myself and opened the door. The room

itself was untouched by the fire. A beautiful mahogany dresser sat on one side and a pristine white vanity with a Victorian-style mirror sat on the other. In the middle of the room was a king-sized bed with hand-carved oak posts and frame. Carefully crafted designs were etched into the wood. It would've been an idyllic scene had it not been for the two unrecognizable dead bodies lying on the bed.

"Is it them?" Little Beth asked innocently from the hallway. "Is it Mommy and Daddy?"

"I don't know," I said despite the high probability. "Stay where you are."

I moved to the side of the bed to get a closer look at the decomposed corpses. The one on left appeared to be the same height as Allie Martin and the one on the right fit the dimensions of Edward. What struck me the most was how they were positioned. They both had their hands neatly folded over their chests as if they had simply gone to sleep. I found it unsettling that Beth would not only have them lying that way but also that there was no apparent struggle. One would assume from their presentation that they welcomed it.

I stepped out into the hallway and knelt beside Little Beth. "I think it's them," I told her softly.

Tears welled in her eyes. "Can I see them?"

"Of course," I said. After all, they were already in her head like that. What good would keeping her out do? "I'll go in with you."

We eased into the room. She kept her distance but suddenly didn't seem as upset. She moved over to the mahogany dresser and opened a drawer. She took out a neatly folded quilt and carried it to the bed. She spread the quilt over their bodies, leaving their heads uncovered. She stood close to the bed, smiling as she stared at them. That moment felt eeriest of all.

"Mommy quilted it herself," she said. "She was going to show me how but never got the chance. At least now, they won't catch cold."

She moved toward me and wiped a single tear from her cheek. "We can go," she said. "They're at peace."

Before I could respond, not that I had formulated a response that I considered particularly productive, there was a crash in the kitchen. Little Beth grabbed my arm tightly, her unexpected acceptance giving way to fright. I held my finger to my lips for her to be quiet. Holding her hand, we slowly and silently made our way down the hall to see what had made the sound. When we reached the kitchen, we found Allie and Edward Martin, alive and in the flesh. They were the age they would've been when Beth was a child.

"Beth?" Allie said when she saw her daughter. She ran to her and hugged her closely. "Thank God, you're alright!"

"We heard a noise," said Little Beth.

"That was your father," Allie explained. "He was going to tear this place apart to find you."

Edward approached Little Beth and rubbed her head like a puppy dog. "Hey, sweetheart. We were worried sick about you."

"I don't understand," said Little Beth. "If you're here, who is that in the bedroom?"

"What in heavens are you talking about?" asked Allie.

"I'll show you," said Little Beth.

She took Allie by the hand and led her out of the kitchen. Edward and I followed closely behind. He glanced at me, smiled, and then looked away. While Allie seemed the same, only younger, Edward didn't have the "lost in thought" look in his eyes he did in real life at his actual age. I wondered at what point his mind started to go and about the accuracy of Beth's current depiction of him.

Little Beth entered the room first. "See!" she said, indicating the bodies.

"Oh, my," Allie said, moving near the bed. "This is quite peculiar." She studied the uncovered heads and turned to Edward. "What do you make of this, dear?"

Edward rubbed his chin in the doorway. "I can't make hide nor hair of it," he said. "Take off that blanket so we can get the full picture."

Allie whipped the quilt off the couple. They were now wearing clothes. The female had on a farm dress like Little Beth's except in an adult size. The male wore a black suit and tie. Both outfits were unwrinkled and pristine compared to the bodies inside them. Allie noticed a necklace on the female and examined it. She walked over to Little Beth and put her arm around her.

"I don't know how to say this, sweetheart," said Allie. "But it's you."

"Me?!" Little Beth began to breathe heavily. "How is that *me*?!"

"Well, that's your dress. Isn't it?" she said in a calm, unsettling tone. "And look here…"

She pointed to a charm on the necklace. "It says Elizabeth."

Little Beth began to sob. "I-I-I don't understand," she said.

"There, there," Allie consoled her. "It happens to all of us eventually. Your time just came sooner than expected."

"B-b-but if that's me…" Little Beth said, crying uncontrollably. She motioned toward the male body. "Who's that?"

"Let me take a gander," said Edward. He moved to the corpse and gave it a once-over. He nodded knowingly and then turned to me and smiled. "That's you, Max."

I jolted out of Beth's mind and back into the uncomfortable chair in her hospital room. I wasn't sure if it was her strong emotional reaction that pushed me out or mine. Either way, the whole scene had enough nightmare-like qualities to warrant waking up from it. Only Beth didn't have that luxury. She couldn't escape and would continue to face whatever her unconscious laid out for her. I hoped that she had moved on to more pleasant thoughts. But then the monitors tracking her vital signs began to beep loudly.

Two nurses entered the room and checked the monitors. "Her heartrate is accelerated," one of them said. "I'm going to need you to step outside."

I quickly got up from the chair and stepped out into the hallway. "Will she be okay?" I asked.

"We're going to do what we can," the other nurse answered and then shut the door in my face.

I stood out in the hallway while the nurses attempted to calm Beth down. She'd already been through intense physical and mental trauma. Further anguish would be difficult for anyone to endure. I wanted badly to go into the room and project again, just so I could tell her everything would be okay. I couldn't bear the thought of her younger self experiencing more horrors or possibly encountering her older self's attacker.

After several minutes, the nurses emerged from the room. "She's stabilized," one of them said. "We'll have an on-call doctor check in with her later, but you can go back in for now."

They headed down the hallway together and I stepped into the room. I sat down across from Beth and glanced at the vital sign monitors. Everything was as it was before, quiet and steady. I wondered if they'd given her medication through an IV or if she'd found her own way out of an increasingly stressful situation. Wanting to see for myself, I entered her mind without further hesitation.

I materialized outside of the "retirement" hotel, right by the front door. I tried opening it, but it was locked. I looked around for Beth, but she was nowhere to be seen. A thick mist that hadn't been there before bordered the imaginary property lines. I walked down the neatly manicured sidewalk and stopped at the edge of the hazy wall. When I reached out to touch it, it resisted my finger like a force field.

Chapter Fourteen

A similar phenomenon occurred during dream work. Quite often, a static barrier would appear, preventing me from being able to go further. I call it a dream peripheral, as it represents the outskirts of the context in which the dream takes place. Only in Beth's case, the obstruction was added rather than having existed from the beginning. It was as if her mind had initially offered the possibility of going beyond the "retirement" hotel and now closed it in so there was no escape.

I walked the perimeter of the imaginary property and discovered that the dense wall of fog did indeed fence in the entire place. It even went so far as the end of the golf course, where any one working on their swing would find that the ball would only bounce back to them like a boomerang. But there was no one on the imaginary golf course. Nor was there anyone sitting on the veranda of the imaginary restaurant. Beth had either sent them away or hid them somewhere.

I checked the back entrance through the veranda and discovered that it was locked as well.

I suddenly heard AC/DC coming from inside a patch of forest within the golf course. I cautiously moved toward the repeating chorus of "Highway to Hell." When I reached the trees, I pushed my way through some branches and came upon a clearing. A Ford pickup truck was in the middle of the clearing. The music blared through the stereo speakers and out the open windows. A resurrected Charlie headbanged near the truck while Teenage Beth sat on the lowered tailgate and took a swig from a bottle of Jack Daniel's. Another teenage girl and a guy who looked twice their ages were lying in the bed of the truck behind Teenage Beth and kissing.

Teenage Beth saw me as I approached her. "Oh, it's you!" she shouted over Angus Young's guitar, her eyes glazed over. She took another drink of whiskey. "I want to apologize for turning into a monster and trying to kill you!"

"Don't worry about it!" I yelled back and then motioned to Charlie. "Looks like he came out of it okay too!"

"It takes a lot to stop Charlie! Once we sewed his head back on, he was as good as new!"

She held the bottle out for me to take, her eyelids drooping to slits. "You want some?!"

"No, thanks!" I pointed toward the "retirement" hotel. "I was hoping you could get me inside!"

"I'm not going back in there! Too much freaky shit going on!"

"All you'd have to do is get me in!"

The song came to an abrupt stop. Charlie ceased giving himself whiplash and came over to me. The older guy in the truck leapt out and joined him. He had a crewcut, a sleeveless white t-shirt and a tattoo down his arm that said "Kick Ass. Ask Questions Later." The words were encircled by a snake. The fact he could have been their father made him look a little ridiculous.

The other girl that was with him in the truck sat up beside Teenage Beth on the tailgate. She wore a Mötley Crüe t-shirt cut off at her belly and blue jean shorts.

"I believe the lady told you 'no,'" said Charlie.

"Don't you remember me, Charlie?" I asked. "We smoked pot together."

"Not really," he answered. "Everything's been kind of blurry since I had my head reattached."

"Look," I persisted. "All I want is to get inside the hotel."

"Then do it on your own, hoss," spoke the other guy.

"Believe me, I would," I said. "But I don't think I can do it without Beth's help."

The other guy grabbed my shirt collar like we were in high school and pulled my face toward his. "I think you'd better leave," he scowled. "Nobody wants you here."

"Let him go," slurred Teenage Beth.

He let go of my shirt collar but kept glaring at me. "Alright," he said. "But just say the word and I'll kick his ass."

"You'll have to excuse Earl," continued Teenage Beth. "He just got out of prison last week and has been looking for a brawl ever since." She stood up between us, drunkenly wobbling back and forth. "Which gives me an idea." She patted my chest. "I'll help you..." She turned to Earl and patted his chest. "But you gotta fight Earl first."

"Excuse me?"

"If you win," she continued. "I'll go with you. But if Earl wins, I stay here, and you go away forever."

Earl's eyes lit up. "Hell, yeah!" He peeled off his shirt and exposed another tattoo on his bare chest off a bikini-clad cartoon woman straddling an inflight nuclear missile. "Let's go, ya sumbitch!"

"Sorry to disappoint you, but I'm not going to fight you," I told him.

"Then I ain't goin' anywhere," Teenage Beth said and then plopped back down on the tailgate.

She obviously wasn't going to budge. I had no idea why she wanted me to fight him.

The best I could figure was that she had entered an anger stage and Earl represented a desire to lash out because of her circumstances. I guess it didn't really matter. I couldn't get back to her adult self without her assistance, so I decided to play along. After all, none of it was real.

"Okay," I agreed. "I'll fight him."

"Woohoo!" cried out the other girl. She leapt off the tailgate and gave Earl a sloppy kiss. "You got this, baby!"

"This is gonna be good," said Charlie.

Everyone stepped aside except for Earl and sat on the edge of the tailgate. He stood about three feet away from me, popping his neck and shaking his hands out like we were in professional boxing ring. He definitely outsized me, but I had the power of manipulation in my corner. I had imposed my will inside dreams many times before. I didn't see how this would be any different.

"So, what are the rules?" I asked.

"There are no rules," replied Teenage Beth.

"So how do we know who won?" I inquired.

"Whoever isn't dead," Teenage Beth replied.

"Hell, yeah!" laughed the other girl.

"Enough yapping!" said Earl. He got into a fighting stance with his fists raised. "Let's go!"

He swung at me, but I ducked. He tried an upper cut, but I caught his fist midair. I squeezed his hand and willed it to turn into an orange. He stepped away from me with a look of shock on his face. He held up the piece of fruit now attached to his wrist and the others gasped. Earl tried shaking the orange off, but it was stuck to him like a new appendage. He attempted to pull it off with his remaining hand, but it was no use.

"Dude," said Charlie. "I gotta stop smokin' so much weed."

Now mad as hell, Earl let out a war cry and charged at me. I moved out of the way and he ran into a tree. He came at me a second time, but I willed a Dobermann Pinscher to appear.

The imaginary dog attacked Earl and knocked him to the ground. It pounced on him and bit into his arm, causing him to scream. Blood spewed from the open gash. The animal went for his face, but I made it vanish right before it tore into his flesh again. Earl scrambled around on the ground and found his t-shirt. He wrapped the garment around the wound to stop the bleeding.

"Well?" I said to Teenage Beth. "Is that good enough for you?"

She scowled at me. I had seen that look before. It was the same look Katie gave me when I grounded her unfairly or gave her a half-assed version of the truth. She knew what I was doing and wasn't going to let me get away with it. She focused on Earl as he applied pressure to his injury and then turned her attention back to me. Her facial expression shifted to an equally familiar one. She smiled smugly.

"Get up, Earl," she said, keeping her eyes on me.

"I just got bit by a dog!" he shouted. "I'm bleeding!"

"You're not bleeding," she said. "And there was no dog. Was there, Max?"

"You don't believe me?!" Earl said before I could respond.

"Look!" He removed the shirt from his arm and the laceration had disappeared, blood and all. The orange attached to his wrist had also changed back into his hand. "How'd you do that?!"

"Whoa," said Charlie. "It's like sorcery or some shit."

"Now, stand up..." Teenage Beth said to Earl. "And finish him."

Earl slowly got up off the ground. As he rose to his feet, he gradually expanded into a giant. Initially around six foot two with a medium build, he now stood five stories high with a proportionately enormous body. He let out a hearty, bellowing laugh that shook the trees and made the earth tremble. Charlie and the other girl grabbed onto the tailgate to brace themselves as the truck vibrated.

"Damn, babe!" said the other girl. "Is *everything* bigger now?!"

"Oh, yeah!" he said in a loud, booming voice. He reached down his human-sized hand and picked me up off the ground. He held me about six feet from his face. "I got you now, little man!"

"What are you going to do?" I asked calmly. "Eat me?"

"I don't eat dudes!" he roared, making the others chuckle down below. "I think I'll just..." He started to squeeze me tightly. "Crush you like a fly!"

"A fly, huh?" I said as he squashed me. "That's not a bad idea."

I transformed into a fly and flew out of his hand. I buzzed around his head, causing him to swat at me. Barely missing getting smacked by his huge palm, I dove into his right ear. He stuck his gigantic finger in after me. He dug in deep trying to catch me, but I escaped his efforts.

I went further inside his head to find nothing but a thin layer of static electricity, not surprisingly since Beth's field of vision didn't go beyond his outside physical characteristics.

"Get out of my head, dude!" shouted Earl.

I shot out of his nose and avoided his feeble attempts to whack me yet again. I aimed for the truck and landed twenty feet or so away from it. I morphed back into myself and watched as Earl checked his surroundings with a "Where did he go,

George?" expression on his face. Teenage Beth hopped off the tailgate and came over with her bottle of Jack Daniel's to join me.

"That all you got?" she asked. "Looks like I win."

"Don't count on it," I said. "I planted a bomb in his brain that's about to detonate."

"You're lying."

"Why do you think I flew out of there so fast?"

"I don't believe you."

"You might want stand back." I took a few steps backward. I glanced at my watch as if I had set a timer. "Three…"

"What's going on?" Charlie asked bewilderedly.

"Yeah," said the other girl, equally as baffled. "Why's he looking at his watch?"

"Two…" I continued.

Earl noticed me. "There you are!" he hollered and then reached down to grab me.

"Three!" I exclaimed.

Earl's head exploded into a million pieces. Everyone's jaw dropped. The rest of Earl came crashing down on top of the truck and several unsuspecting trees. Charlie and the other girl let out screams that were quickly muffled as Earl's giant, headless body flattened them like pancakes. After the scene unfolded before us, Teenage Beth quietly drank a mouthful of whiskey. I wasn't sure if she was planning a counterattack or to curse me for obliterating her companions. Ultimately, she seemed too numb at that point to care either way.

"To hell with it," she said finally. "I'll go with you."

Chapter Fifteen

"You think you're pretty clever. Don't you?" Teenage Beth said as we made our way through the golf course and toward the veranda.

"How do you mean?" I asked.

"You didn't make me believe there was a bomb," she said. "I wanted there to be a bomb."

"And why is that?"

"Because I want all this to go away."

It made sense that Beth's teenage self was predominant at this point. She was definitely the most self-destructive of the three. Sure, Little Beth burned her house down, but she wasn't in it when it happened. And, of course, Adult Beth held a funeral for a cocoon, but that was more about transitioning than the act of dying itself. Teenage Beth, on the other hand, seemed hell-bent on drinking and smoking herself into oblivion.

Once we were on the veranda, she tried opening the door, but it still wouldn't budge. She walked over to one of the restaurant tables and picked up a chair. She hurled the chair at the glass door leading inside but it only ricocheted off the pane and barely missed my head as it flew off the veranda. She looked in through the windows, but the lobby area was still empty. She turned to me and shrugged.

"I don't know what to tell you, dude," she said. "I guess you're out of luck."

"There has to be another way in," I said.

"Well, I can't think of anything." She moved to another table and sat down. "What is it you want in there anyway?"

"Answers."

"You won't find them in there."

"Why not?"

"Because there are none." She took another drink. "You're wasting your time."

I took a seat across from her. "I disagree. I think there's something in there and you're not telling me. You're hiding out here to avoid it. Maybe we can go in and face it together."

She laughed. "Don't psychotherapize me, asshole!"

"I'm not. I just think you're stronger than you give yourself credit for. You turned Earl into a giant. Not anyone can do that."

"You really crack me up, man. You and I both know why I was able to turn that fool into a giant. Same reason you made a dog appear and turned into a fly."

"Why?"

She motioned all around us. "Because none of this is real! The others are just too scared to admit it!"

"You know about the others?"

"The girl from *Little House on the Prairie* and the crazy bitch next door?! Of course, I do! I see them in the hallway all the time."

"You don't recognize them?"

"Should I?"

I wanted to tell her the truth. That she was in a coma and was split between three versions of herself inside her mind. But I didn't. Besides, it wasn't her teenage self that needed to see the light. I had to find her adult self before it was too late. Before I could answer, Charlie appeared and saved me from having to make up a lie. He was completely flat, kind of like in *Tom and Jerry* after one of them gets leveled by a steam roller only to later pop out into a full-sized body again. He swayed back and forth, more cardboard cutout than human.

"Hey, babe," he said through thin, one dimensional lips. "I don't feel so good."

"I told you it takes a lot to stop Charlie," said Teenage Beth, not at all surprised to see him. "But, of course, *he's* not real either."

"He means a lot to you," I said. "Doesn't he?"

"Yeah," she said nostalgically. "We were going to run away

to New York City together. He'd have his band and I'd work at an art gallery."

Flat Charlie fell onto the ground with a light thud. "A little help here?" he said in a muffled voice. "I can't get up on my own."

"Funny how things work out," she continued, ignoring him. "You make a plan and the universe dumps all over it."

"Seriously," said Flat Charlie. "I can't feel my...anything."

"Do you know where he is now?" I probed.

She shook her head. "I don't even know where I am," she said.

I could've told her that he'd died in an accident, but, honestly, what would that have accomplished? Most likely, either it would've upset her, or she wouldn't believe me given her regressive state of mind. She sighed and got up from her seat. She then sat cross-legged on the floor beside him and placed her hand on his forehead, which was really nothing more than the equivalent of a piece of cardstock.

"Shhh," she whispered. "Everything's going to be alright."

"What happened to me?" he asked.

Teenage Beth motioned to me. "This knucklehead made giant Earl's head explode and his body landed on you."

"Oh," he said.

"Don't you think he deserves an apology?" she asked me expectantly.

"Of course," I played along. "Sorry, Charlie."

"It's cool, man," he said. "It definitely gives you a whole new perspective."

"I love you, Charlie," she said. "But it's time for you to go."

"Okay," he said. "Will it hurt?"

"Not at all," she said. "Just close your eyes."

His eyelids closed as if he were in a children's pop-up book and a paper lever had been pulled at the bottom of the page. Teenage Beth slowly waved her hand over him, and, one part of him at a time, he transformed into M&M's. Eventually, there was nothing left of Flat Charlie.

All that remained was his outline, filled in perfectly with hundreds of candy-coated chocolate mini-treats. She picked up a handful and put them in her mouth.

"Man, I miss these," she said, crunching them with her teeth. She rose to her feet and faced me. "You want some?"

"No, thanks," I replied. "I'm more of a Three Musketeers guy."

"Suit yourself. By the way, there may be another way inside. It's a shot in the dark, but it might be worth it."

"Where?"

She took one last drink of Jack Daniel's and wiped the excess from her mouth. "Follow me," she said, slamming the bottle onto the table.

We got down off the veranda and back onto the golf course. I followed her around the side of the "retirement" hotel, and we came upon a ladder leading up to the roof. Mind you, the ladder was no regular ladder. It was made of human bones. For some reason, I began to think she wanted to trick me and was leading me off track. She certainly seemed a little too eager to help me when, mere moments earlier, she said I was wasting my time. She started to climb the ladder and, about halfway up, turned to face me.

"What's wrong?" she asked. "Aren't you coming?"

"What's up there again?"

"I already told you. A possible way in. Look, if you don't want to go up there, that's fine by me. I got M&M's and whiskey waiting for me back at the restaurant. I'm only doing this because I got tired of you asking me so many damn questions."

"Fine," I said and then put my foot on the first rung, which was a femur. "I'll go with you."

"Good," she said smiling.

I climbed the ladder after her and followed her onto the roof. In the center of the roof, there was a swirling vortex of light and color. The ground beneath our feet pulled us toward it. Not one to willingly fall into a pit of unknown origin, I grabbed onto a weather vane. Teenage Beth continued to gravitate toward the cosmic drain. Right as she was about to go in, she turned to me and pouted.

"Don't you trust me?" she said and then got sucked into the vortex.

The weather vane began to bend toward the vacuum. I contemplated pulling out of Beth's mind, perhaps trying again later and discovering that the doors had miraculously opened. But then I remembered that I was in her territory. I was only a visitor and she alone had the power to take me where I needed to go. The weather vane broke off completely and I fell to the ground. I let the flow take me and was enveloped by the vortex.

Once I entered, I slid down a tunnel of the same pattern of light and bright colors. Along the way I noticed mouths in the walls of the cylindrical chute. They all murmured the same thing, but I was going too fast to hear it discernably. When I finally reached the end of the shaft, I was pushed out into a pitch-black area where I was glad to at least hit solid ground. It didn't hurt upon impact but felt cold and slimy. I stood up and looked around for light but there was none coming in from anywhere.

Teenage Beth suddenly lit a match. "You made it," she said, her countenance eerily illuminated but encircled by darkness.

She moved the match away from her face and the end of a torch she was holding instantaneously burst into flames, giving a clearer view of our surroundings. We were inside a cave. This was promising, as caves in dream work often meant a passage-way into a deeper memory and the feelings associated with it. I just hoped she wasn't purposely leading me somewhere insubstantial. I noticed crude drawings on the walls. There was one of a stick figure family, two tall characters and a smaller one standing beside them and wearing a triangle dress.

"The little girl drew those," said Teenage Beth. "Kind of silly if you ask me."

"She's been here?" I asked.

"We all have, but not at the same time. Come on. We're not far from where we're going."

"And where is that?"

"Seriously, if you ask me one more freaking question, I'm going to light myself on fire with this torch. Now let's go."

She led me further down the rabbit hole. Along the way, I noticed a progression in the caveman-like wall sketches. Initially, the family unit was together, but, as we walked, the smaller character was drawn at increasingly longer distances from the taller characters. Eventually, it was the smaller character standing alone. I assumed the sequence represented the inevitable separation of Beth from her parents.

A short while later, Teenage Beth came to a stop. "Here we are," she said. "Now we just wait for him."

Before I could inquire about who "he" was and risk Teenage Beth setting herself ablaze, the older, shabbily dressed man I encountered earlier in Adult Beth's hotel room bathroom appeared before us holding his own torch. He gave us both a once-over, not seeming to recognize either of us. I remembered him asking for a password when I first met him and having no idea what he was talking about.

"Well?" he said impudently.

"2, 6, 7, 21, 31," said Teenage Beth.

"Alright, then," he said. He opened a door behind him that led into Adult Beth's hotel room, the same exact spot where I had originally met him. "Off you go."

I started to enter the dimly lit room but realized Teenage Beth wasn't following me.

"Aren't you coming?" I asked.

She smiled. "You're on your own now, chief," she said. "But if you do happen to get any answers about what the hell all of this means, do me a favor and keep it to yourself."

"Thanks," I told her.

"Don't mention it."

I stepped into the hotel room and the older, shabbily dressed man shut the door in my face. Out of curiosity, I opened it to see if they were still there. Instead of a dark, mysterious cave, I found an empty, ordinary hotel bathroom, complete with fresh towels and neatly packaged hygiene products. I moved further into the room and stopped when I reached the bed.

Beth was lying provocatively on top of the covers wearing a black blindfold and negligee.

"Where have you been?" she asked.

Chapter Sixteen

I walked away from the bed and into the living room area. I suspected she thought I was "Mr. Stevens" or Bobby, so I didn't want to alarm her when she discovered that it was me. I started to speak but remembered my original plan. I shut my eyes and recalled all the details of Margaret's videos and photos on her cell phone. I even replayed the memory Mr. Freeman had of the night she and Bobby came to the office party.

"Where are you going?" she called from the bed. "Don't you want to play?"

Once I had a complete mental picture, or as complete as I could get given the fact I'd never met her face to face, I morphed into Margaret Stevens. I was standing by a mirror in the living room when I changed. When I first saw myself in it, I flinched. No matter how often I did it, transforming into someone else always made me feel uneasy. I was wearing the same clothes she wore to the office party.

"I'm not—" I began to speak but realized it was still my voice.

"You okay, honey?" said Beth from the bed. "You're not still sick. Are you? You don't sound like yourself."

I ran the videos through my head again. This time I had it. "I'm not who you think I am," I said in Margaret's voice.

Beth got off the bed and took off the blindfold. "What are you doing in here?" she asked.

She flipped on the lights and froze when she saw me standing before her as Margaret. "It's you. You're not welcome here. I want you to leave."

"Who is it you think that I am?" I asked.

"Don't play innocent, sweetheart," she said. "You know who you are, and you know what you did. I can't believe you'd have the audacity to show your face."

"I'm sorry," I said. "What is that I did?"

"Are you playing games or just stupid? You tried to steal my husband!"

"I did?" I said, not having to pretend to be confused.

"Yes! But I got news for you. He doesn't love you! In fact, he can't stand the sight of you! Now get out of our lives before I get really angry! Is that clear enough for you?!"

"By 'you,' do you mean Margaret?"

"I'm Margaret, you dumb whore!"

"No. I'm Margaret. I'll prove it to you."

I willed an imaginary purse to appear on the coffee table next to me. I perused through it as I surmised a woman might and pulled a wallet out of a variety of items including lipstick, towelettes, and granola bars. I opened the wallet to a driver's license I conjured and showed it to Beth. It had Margaret's picture and address on it. Beth studied it for a moment and then knocked the wallet out of my hand.

"That's obviously a fake!" she said. "Now get out of here!"

"Listen," I said. "I know this is a lot for you to take right now. I'm not trying to upset you. But there's something I need to tell you."

"I don't want to hear it," she whispered.

"Your name is Beth Martin and you're in a—"

"I said I don't want to hear it!" she shouted and stormed out of the room.

When she got into the hallway, she froze in her tracks. She saw something that made her turn around and come back into the room. She sat down on the couch in the living room area, looking frightened. I walked out into the hallway to see what had affected her so much. Sitting on the floor by "Room 7," Little Beth had her head down and held her face in her hands. I stepped back into the room and Beth looked at me pleadingly.

"Is she gone?" she asked like she'd just seen the boogeyman.

"I'm afraid not," I said. "You're in a coma, Beth. I hate to tell you this way, but I need your help."

"I told you. I'm Margaret."

"Neither of us is Margaret." I morphed into myself. "Margaret's dead," I said with my own voice.

"It's you. How did you do that?"

"Where we are it's pretty easy. This is all happening inside your head. You've been telling yourself you're Margaret but you're not." I conjured up another driver's license.

"Look…" I showed her a picture of herself. "This is you. Beth Martin." I pointed to her address.

"That's where you live. Your parents are Edward and Allie Martin."

She took the license out of my hand and stared at it intently. She got up from the couch and saw herself in the mirror. She compared her reflection to the photo on the ID. As if she'd had an epiphany, she dropped the license to the floor. She realized she was scantily clad and covered herself with her hands. She rushed into the bathroom and shut the door behind her. I didn't know whether she'd come out or disappear into another dimension. Fortunately, she came out a few seconds later wearing a bathrobe. She walked back to the couch and sat down again. I gave her a moment. After all, it was a hell of a lot to process.

"So, none of this is real?" she asked.

"No," I answered.

"Are you real?"

"Yes."

"How did you get here?"

"I projected into your mind. I'm a psychic."

"That seems kind of intrusive. Doesn't it?"

"It was the only way to talk to you."

"What about that little girl in the hall? Is she real?"

"She was."

"She's me. Isn't she?"

"She's your younger self."

"And Margaret? Is she really dead?"

"Yes."

"How did she die?"

"She committed suicide."

"Oh, my God. How long have I been in a coma?"

"Two weeks."

I sat down in an empty chair across from her. I knew the situation was delicate but couldn't tell how much. There was always a chance she might have a negative reaction and turn into the crimson creature again. I made sure to maintain a calm demeanor, the way one would with a fragile child that breaks down when he or she feels helpless or threatened. She appeared in control, but I didn't want to take any chances.

"Did you pretend to be my husband?" she inquired.

"I did. Your parents as well."

"Why?"

"I was hoping to trigger something that might help you realize who you really were. It didn't work very well."

"I suppose not. So that was you I kissed on the veranda?"

I tried to maintain a professional composure and not blush. "It was." I felt my face turn red despite my efforts. "I'm sorry about that. I shouldn't have misled you."

"Somehow I knew all along. I wanted to believe you were him just like part of me wanted to believe I was Margaret."

"Why would you want to be Margaret?"

She hesitated. "She and Bobby were having an affair," she said finally. "It had been going on for as long as we were engaged. Maybe longer. I was going to confront him about it but...I can't remember if I did or not. I guess I wasn't ready to accept that it was over."

"So, when I looked like Margaret and you said I tried to steal your husband, you really meant fiancé?"

"I guess so."

"Would Bobby try to have you killed?"

"No! Why would you ask that?!"

"You were attacked and left for dead on the way back to Louisville from your parents' house. Do you remember that at all?"

"No."

"That's why you're in a coma. I came here to find out who did it."

"Bobby's a liar and a cheater, but he isn't a murderer. Are you sure I wasn't in an accident?"

"I'm positive. They discovered you in a field off the highway. You'd been beaten."

"Who would've done that?"

"I don't know. I thought maybe you had some ideas."

She ruminated for a moment. "Damnit. I just realized I missed my deadline."

"What deadline?"

"I'm a curator at an art gallery in Louisville. I was supposed to make a proposal to the directors."

"I'm sure they'll understand."

"Not these people. They're real assholes." She sprung up from the couch. "So how do I get out of here?"

"Listen, I realize this is a lot to take in. Maybe we should focus on who tried to kill you for now."

"Alright. Fine. Get me out of here, and we'll figure it out together."

"I appreciate your eagerness, but it's not that simple."

"Sure, it is. I'll just wake up, and we can retrace my steps. Maybe I could remember something."

"I don't think you can just wake yourself up. You're in pretty bad shape."

"Sure, I can."

Beth went to the door and stepped outside. I followed her into the hallway. Her younger self was no longer sitting in the hallway. She marched down the hall and into the lobby area.

There were actually people again but nothing quite like the time when I had to chase down the imaginary priest that was going to perform a funeral service for a human-sized cocoon. Beth stormed the front desk.

"I want to wake up," she told the man behind the counter.

"I'm sorry," he said. "You want to what?"

"Wake up," she repeated.

"Are you sleepwalking?" he asked.

"No. As a matter of fact, I'm very much alert right now."

"I think what she's saying is," I chimed in, "she's ready to check out."

"Oh, of course," he said. "Allow me to review your record." He started typing quickly into a keyboard attached to a table top computer. "Oh, no. You can't check out. It says here your stay is indefinite."

"Are you sure? Check it again. My name's Beth Martin."

He smiled at her sympathetically and then turned the computer monitor so we could see it. "You see." He pointed to her name in black letters on an otherwise white screen. Next to her name it said, "Permanent Resident." "I'm afraid my hands are tied on this one."

She turned to me. "Can't you do something?"

"What is it you want me to do?"

"You said you projected into my mind. Can't you take me with you when you leave?"

"It doesn't work that way."

"Well, there has to be *something*!" She moved away from the desk and saw Grilax and Grulax, the two half-human, half-alien "security guards" standing near the front door. "I've seen them before. What the hell are they?"

I saw no reason not to be completely honest with her. "When you thought we were Mr. and Mrs. Stevens, you told me we made them together," I answered.

"I said that?! I don't remember saying that!"

She hurried past me and nearly knocked down an older woman using a walker. I turned around to see that Grilax and Grulax were watching us. I gave them a thumbs up, hoping that would keep them at bay. It didn't. They moseyed toward me on their tentacles as Beth pushed the door open onto the veranda. I went out to meet her. A familiar waiter approached her as she frantically looked around for an exit strategy.

"Would you like your regular table, madam?" he asked.

"Hell, no!" she told him as she strode over to the end of the veranda and surveyed the golf course. "There has to be a way out of here!"

The waiter saw me and cleared his throat. "Hello, sir. Do you have a reservation?"

"I'm with her," I replied, motioning to Beth.

"Of course, you are," he said and then walked away.

Grilax and Grulax appeared at the door. The few patrons at the restaurant took cover under their tables when they saw them as if they were in a western and a gunfight was about to occur. I went over to Beth with the intention of trying to calm her down. Grilax and Grulax followed close behind. I held up my finger asking them for a moment before they treated us like a security issue. I'd already been ejected once. I didn't want it to happen again.

"They're going to throw us out if you don't tone it down a little," I told her.

"That's what I want them to do!" She turned around to face the creatures. "Go ahead! Throw me out, you octopus wannabes!"

Grilax and Grulax glanced at each other and shrugged. They shuffled over to us but only grabbed hold of me. They began to pull me away from Beth, trying to drag me toward the lobby area. Beth shoved them off me, and they both let out high-pitched, pig-like squeals. They slowly went back inside like two dogs with their tails between their legs. Or, in this case, tentacles.

"You see!" she said. "They were going to throw *you* out! Not me! I'm stuck here!"

She whisked past me and ran down the steps to the ground below. She zigzagged across the golf course and stopped when she came to the static barrier enclosing the whole place. I caught up with her as she stood before it bewilderedly. She tried pushing through it, but it resisted her touch the same as it had with me earlier. She even kicked it, but her foot bounced off and she nearly toppled over onto the ground.

"What the hell is it?" she asked.

"Something you built with your mind," I answered.

"Why would I do that?"

I shrugged. "Maybe it's protecting you from something."

"Fine! I'll just make it go away!" She closed her eyes tightly. After a few seconds, she opened them, but the force field remained. "Damnit!"

"There might be another option."

"To make me wake up?!"

"No. To get you out of this place. If your mind is holding you hostage, perhaps we can trick it into releasing you."

"How?"

"By becoming someone else."

Chapter Seventeen

If there was one thing my prior dream work with inmates taught me, it was that, with the right tools, a person could overcome almost anything. Quite often, one of the biggest obstacles to a convict reliving his crime was the innate fear that he wouldn't be able to handle it.

Even the toughest would cower when confronted with their past, particularly the ones that denied it adamantly in the present. More times than not, I had to get creative to help them face the truth.

In Beth's case, I felt she needed to step outside of herself, a task that she had proved capable of doing with the whole Margaret fiasco. By temporarily becoming someone else, she would be able to take on a more detached perspective of the horribleness that occurred to her and hopefully move beyond the "retirement" hotel. Getting her out would serve two purposes.

First of all, it could possibly lead her to a place where she might remember who tried to kill her.

Secondly, we could explore other settings that might help trigger that terrible memory. Before we could even get to that point, however, I first had to teach her the art of shapeshifting.

We acted like everything was hunky dory and headed back to her room. I nodded to Grilax and Grulax on our way, and they reciprocated. The man behind the check-in counter noticed us and then turned his attention to someone else. The important thing was to keep any restrictive elements in check so, when we were ready, we could just walk out the front door.

When we reached her room, she hesitated before going inside. She walked a little way down the hall and came to the door with number "7" on it. She knocked.

"What are you doing?" I asked.

"I need to talk to her before I go. To me, I mean. Tell her everything is going to be okay."

"You just did."

"It's not the same. I can feel her hurting."

No one answered. She knocked again. After waiting a few seconds, she opened the door. A huge gust of wind blew from inside and out into the hallway. She shivered. She stepped inside, and I followed her. Snow fell from the ceiling, flew about, and landed on the already well-covered ground. There was no furniture, only a small tent in the center of the room. Beth's feet crunched the ice beneath her as she approached the tent. She peeked inside to find Little Beth sitting and crying.

"Hi," she said.

"Hi," said Little Beth.

"Can I come in?"

"Sure."

Beth went in and sat down. "Do you mind if my friend joins us?" She motioned to me.

"This is Max."

Little Beth saw me. "I know Max. He helped me bury my dog."

"Really?" asked Beth. "Which one?"

"Petey," I said and then took a spot on the floor inside the tent.

Beth's face lit up. "I remember Petey! What ever happened to that dog?"

"I killed him," said Little Beth. She buried her face in her hands. "I stabbed him with a kitchen knife."

"Oh, no, sweetheart," said Beth. "You wouldn't do something like that."

"Yes, I would," said Little Beth. "I'm evil."

"Why would you say that?" Beth reached out to touch Little Beth's shoulder, but an abrupt burst of static appeared and pushed her hand back. "What was that?!"

"Some form of electric barrier, I suppose," I said. "Maybe you can talk to her but you can't touch her."

"Well, that's stupid!" Beth contested. "Look, honey. Take it from me. You're not evil. I don't know where you got that idea from, but it's not true. Petey...ran away. That's what dogs do."

Little Beth's expression shifted from sadness to anger. "No!" she shouted. "That's what Mommy and Daddy said, but they lie!"

Beth tried to touch her again to console her, but the electrical force field prevented her from being able to do so. Wanting to help, I held my hand out for Little Beth to take. She was still upset, so, when she first saw it, she didn't budge. But, once she let herself calm down a little, she slowly put her hand out toward me. Beth watched in awe as her younger self intertwined her fingers with mine.

"How did you do that?" asked Beth.

"The barrier must only be with you," I said. "Maybe there's something about our friend here that you can't access." I squeezed Little Beth's hand. "I'm sorry about Petey. I know he was a good dog. But you didn't kill him. You're a good girl."

"How do you know?" asked Little Beth.

"Because I can see it in your eyes. Trust me. I'm an expert. I've worked with a lot of bad people. You're not one of them."

She smiled. "Thank you."

"You're welcome." I turned to Beth and saw tears in her eyes. "What's wrong?"

"Nothing," she said. "I can feel her being comforted." She wiped a tear from her cheek. "It's nice." She looked at me a moment and then shook her head. "Just my luck. I finally meet a good guy, and he's only in my head."

The tent levitated above our heads and then disintegrated. The snowstorm around us disappeared as well. Now we were in a regular hotel room again. Sunlight crept in through the window. Little Beth gave my hand a squeeze and let go of it. She got up and moved to the window. She looked out and the landscape of her childhood home appeared on the horizon. Beth rose to her feet and joined her.

"It really is a beautiful place," said Beth.

"Yes," agreed Little Beth.

As they stood together gazing at the picturesque view of the farm house, the sun mysteriously vanished behind the clouds. It became very dark. Both of them seemed confused.

And then the house burst into flames. Little Beth started screaming. Beth tried to touch her again. This time the shock was so powerful it knocked her to the ground. I quickly jumped up and went toward Little Beth. Before I could make my own attempt to help, she too caught fire.

I grabbed Beth by the hand and pulled her to her feet. I wasn't sure what was happening, but I didn't want to risk her regressing in some way. I pulled her away from Little Beth and toward the door. The walls of the room now burned as well. Beth resisted me, wanting to go to Little Beth. I forced her to come with me and soon we were back out in the hallway. I shut the door.

"Let me back in there!" she shouted, jerking away from me. "She's in pain!"

I stood between her and the door. "It's not real, Beth," I said. "You have to tell yourself it's not real and it'll stop."

"But it *feels* real!"

"It's all in your mind. You're having an emotional reaction to something you're creating."

"Yeah? Well, it's not like a dream where I can just wake up. Is it?"

She walked back to her room and went inside. I lingered in the hall for a moment, wanting to give her some time to recompose. I had never second guessed myself with anyone I'd worked with as much as I did with Beth. Perhaps it was the fact that the others were criminals and the line was clearer as to what was right or wrong. In her case, I'd make a decision and often regret it immediately afterwards. I stepped inside the room and shut the door behind me.

Beth sat on the couch in the living room area.

"I'm sorry," I told her. "I shouldn't have pulled you out of there like that."

"Thank you," she said. "I'm a big girl. I can handle things."

I took the chair across from her. "You're right. It's not my place to try to protect you."

"I don't even know you. Are you a therapist? You definitely talk like a therapist."

"I'm a specialist working with the FBI."

"How did they get involved?"

"An agent I've collaborated with in the past found out about you and asked for my help."

"So, what do you do outside of people's minds?"

"I have a family. My wife, Jessica and our daughter, Katie."

"Do they have special powers?"

"It seems my daughter has inherited them from me. She's having a hard time dealing with it. Along with all the other stuff teenagers have to deal with in this day and age."

"To be honest with you, I used to think the whole psychic thing was nonsense."

"And now?"

She pointed to me. "Either you're a well-crafted figment of my imagination or I really should've listened to that palm reader at the state fair."

People's perceptions of psychics tend to fall into two categories. If it wasn't a stereotypical image of a head-scarf–wearing gypsy sitting behind a crystal ball and flipping tarot cards, it was a nicely dressed, self-proclaimed expert on television with a 1-800 number and a $9.95/ten minute minimum. It made sense. After all, society has perpetuated those ideas for years.

I chuckled. "I assure you that I'm not a figment of your imagination," I told her. "I've never read anybody's palm either, although I'm sure it's quite lucrative."

She smiled. "So, what's your plan, Max? How are you gonna get me out of here?"

"We're going to walk out the front door. Just not as ourselves."

Teaching someone to morph into someone else can't be compared to, let's say, teaching them to ride a bike. It takes a lot of non-conventional reasoning, some of which contradicts common sense altogether. Getting Beth to learn the skill proved understandably difficult. First, I had to break through her belief that she couldn't be anyone but herself, an ego-driven notion that required eradication before we could move to the next step.

"Who will we be?" she asked.

"Anyone" I replied. "But you have to truly become that person. Otherwise, you're not fooling anyone but yourself."

"I don't think I can do it."

"Why not? You thought you were Margaret."

"That's different. I was still..." She motioned to her face. "Me. Besides, I wasn't aware I was doing it."

"But you still did it. Therefore, on some level, you're capable of letting yourself go."

"Alright, Mr. Smarty Pants. Let's say I was willing to give it a try. Who would I be?"

"I don't know. Think of someone you remember well enough to make yourself look and sound exactly like them."

She ruminated for a moment. A glow fell over her face as if lightbulb turned on above her head, and then she laughed. "I got it!" she said. "Miss Schneiderfelt!"

"Who?"

"She was my third-grade teacher. I can remember everything about the old hag."

"Okay. Miss Schneiderfelt it is. I'll be Mr. Schneiderfelt."

"There was no Mr. Schneiderfelt. She never married. She did live with a lot of cats if that tells you anything."

"Fine. I'll think of someone else then. The important thing is that you have someone in mind. Now we have something we can work with. I want you to close your eyes."

She closed her eyes, only to open one slightly. "Sorry," she said and then shut it again.

"I just wanted to make sure you were still here. I'm ready."

"I want you to picture Miss Schneiderfelt's nose. Only her nose."

She snorted. "Okay."

"Now I want you imagine her nose at the end of your face. All of its little details."

"Okay."

"Now I want you to will her nose to replace your nose."

"Okay."

She closed her eyes more tightly. For a second, nothing happened. And then a pig snout appeared where her nose used to be. She quickly opened her eyes and felt around on her face. When she realized she had a pig snout she jumped up and looked at herself in the mirror on the wall. She started laughing.

She turned to me and covered it as if she became embarrassed by it.

"Sorry," she said. "Miss Schneiderfelt kind of reminded us all of a pig. I guess I thought of a pig at the last second."

"It's okay," I told her. "This is all trial and error. Close your eyes again."

She shut her eyes and put her hands by her sides. "Okay."

"Now focus on Miss Schneiderfelt's nose. Don't think about a pig or any other animal."

She chuckled. "Okay."

Seconds later, an older, larger nose appeared on her face in place of her regular one. She opened her eyes and looked in the mirror. She burst into laughter at the sight of her third-grade-teacher's schnoz contrasted with her normal features. It was quite a funny sight. As much as I attempted to maintain a professional demeanor, I couldn't help but snicker.

"Hey!" she said, still giggling. "It's okay for me to laugh, but not you!"

"Sorry," I said, recomposing myself. "I know it's strange at first, but you'll get used to it."

She inspected her new nose closely in the mirror and flared her nostrils. "I don't think I'd ever get used to this thing."

"That's only the beginning. You have her whole body to do."

Piece by piece, Beth changed into her third-grade teacher, Miss Schneiderfelt. Each new part brought on a similar reaction, and, at times, she couldn't contain herself. But, after becoming accustomed to the process, she eventually had no trouble transforming and appearing to be what I'd assume Miss Schneiderfelt would look like. She stood in front of the mirror and admired her work.

"Not bad," she said in her own voice.

"Just one more thing," I said. "How did Miss Schneiderfelt sound?"

"I don't know. Like an old lady that listens to Pat Boone."

"That's not enough. You have to recall her voice in your mind. That way you can emulate it."

"Okay. Let me think back." She paused for a moment and a smile crept across her, I mean, Miss Schneiderfelt's face. "There was this one time a few of us got in trouble for going to the library without permission. When we saw her coming down the hallway and ran away from her to the girls restroom. We hid in the stalls, but she came in after us. I can still remember what she said to us. 'Girls! Get out of the stinkin' bathroom and back to the classroom before I call your parents!' We laughed so hard I almost peed my pants."

"That's good. Now think hard about *how* she spoke. If you want to convince them you're not Beth and you don't belong here, you have to believe it yourself."

She cleared her throat and recited the line about the "stinkin bathroom." At first, she said it in a high-pitched squeak, almost like a child on the cusp of puberty. She tried it again and a deep, man's voice came out of her mouth. Finally, after trial and error, she was able to mimic Miss Schneiderfelt. Or at least what she told me she sounded like. How would I know? I never met the lady.

"Now what?" she asked with her new voice and a sense of pride.

"It's my turn to change," I replied. "I'll be Mr. Clampstead, a fellow third-grade teacher."

"So, what's our story?"

"We were staying here for a teachers' conference, but now it's time for us to go home."

I transformed into Mr. Clampstead. He was my third-grade teacher and a really funny guy. Sometimes he would turn around from the chalkboard wearing one of those silly glasses-with-an-attached-big-nose disguises, and all the kids would laugh. I wasn't sure if I got his voice exactly right and I'm sure I made his head bigger than it really was, but it didn't matter. What mattered was that Beth completely settled into the role of Miss Schneiderfelt so that she could forget herself long enough to break free from the confining world she'd created.

We left her room and walked side by side down the hallway. She made a concentrated effort to not look at me because, every time she did, she would start to chuckle. We came into the lobby area and approached the front desk. Luckily, we didn't have to wait very long. The man behind the counter paused for a moment to give us a once-over. I sensed Beth getting nervous.

"We're ready to check out," I told him.

"And you are?" he asked.

"Mr. Clampstead and Miss Schneiderfelt," I replied.

"I see." He typed on his keyboard and looked intently at his screen. "I'm sorry, but I don't see you as registered guests."

I willed our aliases to appear at the bottom of the screen. "Look again," I said authoritatively.

"Ah, yes," he said, noticing my subtle addition. He punched a sequence of keys and then flashed a smile. "You're all set. We hope you have a fantastic day."

"So that's it," Beth said in Miss Schneiderfelt's voice. "We can go?"

The man behind the counter laughed. "Of course! Unless you'd like to extend your stay?"

"No!" Beth and I said together as our alter-egos.

"That won't be necessary," I added. "Thank you for your time."

We stepped away from the counter and made our way to the front door. We passed Grilax and Grulax as we walked outside. So far, so good. We made our way down the stairs of the front porch and onto the sidewalk. I went ahead of Beth, strolling along the winding path as if nothing was out of the ordinary. When we reached the static barrier, we both came to a grinding halt.

"I can't do this," she said sheepishly.

"Yes, you can," I told her. "That wall is for Beth Martin. Not Miss Schneiderfelt. It's time for you to go. You're dying to get back to your twelve cats."

She grinned and closed her eyes. A few seconds later, the fortification disappeared. On the road before us was a brand-new convertible with the top down. She opened her eyes and her face glowed when she saw it the way a child does on Christmas morning when they first see what's under the tree. She looked at me and then went straight to the driver's side and got in. She started the engine with an imaginary key and motioned to the passenger's side.

"I take it you're driving," I joked.

"Yep," she said in her own voice. "Now get in so we can get the hell out of here."

I went around to the passenger's side and got into the car. The radio was on. Beth turned up the volume and "Back in Black" by AC/DC blared from the speakers. As we slowly drove away from the "retirement" hotel and down the road, we transformed back into ourselves. I glanced at the rearview mirror. Standing at the end of the sidewalk and holding up her middle finger, Teenage Beth smiled at me as we escaped.

Chapter Eighteen

Our short journey came to an abrupt stop when an elephant blocked our path. The animal crossed the road and was followed by a parade of clowns, monkeys, a unicyclist, and various other performers. A man on stilts in a multicolored shirt and red and white striped pants waved at us. A bearded lady wearing a tattered dress curtseyed as she passed. Once they made it to the other side, one by one they vanished into thin air. We watched them disappear until the last acrobat in line dematerialized.

"What was that about?" asked Beth.

"I don't know," I replied. "Did you ever go to the circus when you were a kid?"

"My parents took me once, but it didn't have that much of an impression on me."

"Sometimes things make a bigger impression than we realize. Shall we continue?"

Beth pressed the gas pedal and we drove onward. Open farmland stretched out as far as the eyes could see. A row of windmills in the distance rotated in unison. The sky darkened, and day turned into night. A house appeared up ahead. When Beth saw it, she hit the brake and the car came to a screeching halt. The place was a two-story affair with only one light on in an upstairs window.

"What's wrong?" I asked.

"I've seen that house before."

"Do you remember where?"

"No."

"Why don't we take a closer look?"

She shook her head. "I can't. Something's not right."

"What if I went inside and you waited in the car?"

"You're not leaving me outside in the dark!"

"Well, what do you suggest?"

"I say we drive past it and forget we ever saw it."

"Beth, you wanted to find out what happened to you. We're not going to get very far if you ignore the signs."

She pointed toward the house. "You think that's a sign?"

"It could be, but we'll never know if we don't investigate."

She took a deep breath and exhaled. "Fine," she said hesitantly.

She went a little further and pulled up by the side of the house. I got out and waited for her by the car. She finally stepped out and came around to meet me. We walked together toward the house side by side. The light in the upstairs window flickered. She grabbed my arm as if we were watching a horror film and the killer had jumped out of the screen. I coaxed her forward until we arrived at the front door.

It creaked as I opened it, yet another, albeit dated, scary-movie-type occurrence. We moved inside and, not surprisingly, the door slammed behind us. Beth gasped. The entire house was dark save the light emitting from an open door in the upstairs room and the moon shining faintly through the windows. Shrouded in blackness, the furniture in a nearby living room was covered in white sheets that gave off a dim glow and made the couch and sofa set appear like oddly shaped ghosts. A spiral staircase stood directly in front of us. I climbed the steps, and Beth stayed close behind.

We followed along the winding metal railing until we came to a hallway of open rooms on the second floor. Only the one at the end of the hall was illuminated, but its radiance gave the others enough light so we could peek inside them. Through the doorway closest to us, we saw a little girl's room bathed in shadows. A small, white dresser sat in the corner near a set of bunk-beds. On the other side of the room, near the window, there was a dollhouse that looked eerily like the house we were in now.

Before either of us could remark on the resemblance, a tiny light came on in the second floor of the dollhouse. Beth looked at me with a mixture of fear and confusion. I shared a similar sentiment but felt it best to remain calm. I walked down the hall to another room. The inside was exactly like the last, complete with the children's furniture and an uncanny miniature model of the house with the same upstairs light whose life-sized version emanated from a few feet away. I soon discovered that the last unlit room was an exact copy of the first two.

We made our way to the brightened room at the end of the hall and looked inside. It was empty except for a photograph lying in the middle of a beige-carpeted floor. A single uncovered lightbulb shone down on the picture, inviting us to look at it. Beth went ahead of me and picked it up off the ground. She examined it for a second and then handed it to me. It was the image of a smiling young girl, no more than six or seven years old, wearing a white dress with a red apple pattern on it. She was encircled by a hazy fog not unlike the barrier Beth had created around the "retirement" hotel.

"Do you recognize her?" I asked.

"No," she replied. "But I feel like I should. What is all of this?"

There was a sudden crash downstairs. Beth and I exchanged concerned looks. I placed the photograph in the exact spot we had found it, wondering if moving it had caused a disturbance.

Putting it back didn't seem to make a difference because there was another loud bang below. We moved into the hallway. From where we stood, we saw that another light had come on in a first-floor room. We cautiously descended the staircase. When we reached the end, we heard another noise like the sound of glass breaking. We slowly turned the corner toward the newly irradiated room. Inside a full-sized kitchen, the girl from the picture took a plate off a stack on a table and smashed it onto the ground. She wore the same apple patterned dress from the photograph.

She saw us and grabbed another plate. "Well, look who decided to show up!" she said and then hurled it at Beth's head.

Beth ducked, and the dish shattered against the wall. "Who are you?"

"Who am I?!" the girl shouted. "How can you not remember me?!"

She went for another plate, but I acted quickly and willed the rest of the stack to disappear. The girl didn't blink an eye. She went over to a drawer near the sink and opened it.

She retrieved a knife and ran with it poised to attack toward Beth. Beth caught her wrist before she stabbed her. Beth wrestled the blade out of girl's hand, but she kicked Beth in the shin, forcing her to release her grip.

"What is your deal?!" asked Beth, wincing in imaginary pain. "Will you stop trying to hurt me for a minute so I can figure out what the hell is going on?!"

The girl crossed her arms. "Fine!" she said. "But if you can't tell me who I am, I'm going to stick your head in the oven!"

I crouched down at the girl's level. "How do you know *her*?" I asked, motioning to Beth.

"She was supposed to take care of me," replied the girl. "But she's forgotten all about me."

"Take care of you?" said Beth, still puzzled. "Was I your babysitter or something?"

"I don't need a babysitter," said the girl. She sat down in a chair at the table and frowned. "I need a friend," she added and then disappeared.

Beth went to the chair the girl was in and sat down. "I'm so confused," she said. "I have no idea who that was."

I took a seat across from her. "It could be that you created her," I suggested. "But she was so specific about you not remembering her, it makes me think there's a memory lodged in your brain you can't access completely."

"But what?"

I shrugged. "Was she a childhood friend maybe?"

"I don't think so. I would've recognized her." She contemplated for a moment. "Wait a minute. Do you think it was Margaret?"

I shook my head. "I saw pictures of her as a child. Unless you altered her image in your mind somehow."

She was about to share another thought when a rock flew through a window by the table. We both leapt from our chairs and took a step back. The rock landed on the ground near our feet next to shards of broken glass. We looked out the partially shattered pane to see where the rock had come from so abruptly. Standing in the front yard and in his underwear, Bobby swayed back and forth with a bottle of liquor in his hand.

"'Tis the time of mourning!" he shouted. "Only now shall you see the light of truth!"

Beth glanced at me, even more baffled than ever. "What the hell do I do with *that*?"

"Maybe we should go talk to him," I suggested.

Beth threw her hands in the air. "Why not? It's not like this whole experience could get any weirder."

We stepped out of the kitchen and into the entryway. I opened the front door and moved out onto the front porch. Bobby danced around on the grass. Upon closer inspection, the bottle in his hand didn't hold liquor. It appeared to be blood. All around him on the ground were snakes, only they didn't have reptilian heads. They slithered around at his feet, each and every one bearing the face of Margaret.

Beth joined me on the porch and surveyed the scene. "Okay," she said. "It just got weirder."

"Dance the dance of nightly bliss!" exclaimed Bobby as he pounced about and nearly stepped on the cold-blooded creatures surrounding him. "Seal your fate with but one kiss!"

"You weren't an English major at one point," I said to Beth. "Were you?"

"No," she said. "Why?"

"Just curious." I approached Bobby carefully, making sure to keep a safe distance from him and his den of hybrids. "What do you mean by that exactly?" I asked him.

He stopped dancing and glared at me. "If thee doth not know, then the same fate shall fall upon thee!" he said.

He opened the bottle and poured the red liquid on top of his head. It flowed down the front and sides of his face then ran down onto his shirt. The snakes bearing Margaret's face hissed at Beth and me. They got louder and louder as Bobby finished dousing himself with the crimson fluid. He looked directly at Beth and threw the bottle by her feet. It shattered upon impact, causing Beth to jump out of the way of flying shards. Bobby began to laugh maniacally.

Beth covered her ears. "Go away!" she screamed.

Bloody Bobby and his supernatural serpents vanished from sight. Beth brushed past me and hastily made her way to the car. I hurried after and hopped in on the passenger's side right as she climbed into the driver's seat. She started the engine and "Don't Fear the Reaper" by Blue Oyster Cult blared from the speakers. She quickly turned off the radio and drove away from the house.

"So where are we headed?" I asked, ignoring the fact the vehicle was rapidly accelerating.

"I don't care," she said, focused on the road ahead. "Just as long as it's not there."

We continued onward and, for a while, saw nothing on either side of the road but the same extensive farmland we had before. But then a house appeared up ahead. As we got closer, I realized it was the exact house we had left only moments earlier. Beth zoomed past it. A few seconds later, it appeared again. And then again. She kept speeding by, but the house continued to pop up over and over. Eventually there were dozens of them receding into the distance, all with the same light on in the upstairs bedroom.

Chapter Nineteen

Beth inevitably pulled the car off the road and parked on the shoulder. She gripped the wheel tightly, obviously overwhelmed by the tricks her mind was playing on her. I couldn't imagine being trapped inside my own head with nowhere to go except where my subconscious led me. In her case, it was taking her for a spin on a repetitive loop that evidently had no end.

She opened the door, exited the car, then leaned against the hood. I got out and joined her.

"None of this makes any sense," she said exasperatedly. "Why does the house keep popping up?"

"Maybe there's something we overlooked the first time and your mind wants you to revisit it," I suggested.

She shook her head. "I'm not going back in there."

If she wasn't ready to face what lay in store for us, I didn't want to push her. The only problem was that we had come to a standstill. I decided that the only way to move forward was to go back to the outside world and poke around a little. Maybe I could find out more about the girl or why Bobby kept turning up in bizarre ways. I could then return with the knowledge necessary to help her. Leaving her alone was my sole hesitation.

"I need to go for a while," I finally said.

"Why?" she asked apprehensively.

"So, I can be more useful to you in here. I'm running out of ideas."

"Oh, no. You're not leaving me. I can't stay here by myself. What if some other weird shit happens while you're gone?"

"It's psychologically draining for me to project into

someone's mind for an extended period. If I don't take a break, I'll be no good for either of us."

"But if you leave, I could go crazy. You want that on your conscience?"

Recognizing that we had come to a stalemate, I ruminated for a moment. "I have an idea," I told her. "What's your favorite place in the whole world?"

"Don't tell me you're gonna ask me to go to my happy place. I swear to God I'll punch you in the face."

"Okay. Then what's a place that would help you stay sane until I come back? It can be anywhere as long as it doesn't cause you any stress."

She crossed her arms like an obstinate child refusing to play along. "No, thank you." When she realized I wasn't going to yield, she uncrossed them. "Alright, fine." She thought about it. "The beach. Definitely the beach."

"Good. I want you to close your eyes and focus on the beach."

She let out a sigh and shut her eyes. After a few seconds, her brow no longer furrowed, and a slight smile crept across her face. The houses that infinitely lined the road dematerialized and the farmland horizon transformed into a vast ocean. The ground beneath our feet turned into white sand. The darkness above transitioned back into day and the sun crept out from behind the clouds. A seagull flew by in the sky. The convertible vanished, and, in its place, two foldable beach chairs appeared. Beth opened her eyes.

"Wow!" she exclaimed. "I did this?!"

"You did," I confirmed.

She sat down in one of the chairs and motioned to the other. "I conjured one for you too."

"I noticed."

"So, what do you do now? Fly off in a spaceship or something?"

I shook my head. "I'll just disappear."

She nodded. "Come back as soon as you can. Okay?"

"I promise."

"Before you go, I just want you to know how much I

appreciate you. I couldn't have done this alone."

I smiled. "See you soon, Beth."

"You too, Max."

I withdrew from her mind and snapped back into reality in her hospital room. She looked peaceful, so I stepped outside into the hallway. I checked the waiting room for Linden, but he was nowhere to be found. I pulled out my phone and saw that I'd gotten a text from him while I was in Beth's head. In typical Linden fashion, the message was as vague as it was frustrating. All it said was that something had come up and that he'd be in touch shortly.

Not wanting to sit around, I called an Uber and went to Bobby's apartment. Linden wouldn't have advised it, but I figured I might have a better chance of getting him to talk one on one. Besides, who knew how long Linden was going to be? I had the Uber driver wait for me at the front gate while I buzzed Bobby's intercom. After no response, I started to leave. But then his voice came through the speaker.

"Yes?" he said.

"Mr. Fugate?" I said. "It's Max Crawford."

"I told you to leave me alone."

"Yes, sir. You did. However, some things have come to light, and I need to talk to you."

"I've got nothing to say. Don't come here again."

"Beth told me about the affair, Bobby. She told me a lot of things. She really needs our help."

Following a long pause, the gate opened. "Come on in," he said.

The Uber driver left, and I walked to Bobby's apartment building. I stepped into a courtyard with a pool and well-landscaped sitting area. Apartments faced the open space, the first-floor ones with substantially sized porches and the second-level ones with equally large balconies. I climbed the steps to Bobby's second-level residence facing the city and went to the front door. I knocked.

"It's open!" Bobby called from inside.

I noticed the door was ajar and pushed it the rest of the way. I moved into the apartment and through the entryway. I came upon the living room, which, on any other day, probably exuded wealth and good taste. On this particular day, however, the open, half-empty pizza box on the coffee table, dirty clothes strewn all over the floor, and pile of beer bottles made it more like a frat house the morning after a particularly decadent party. Bobby was nowhere to be seen.

"Mr. Fugate?" I inquired.

He hurriedly entered the room and tackled me against the wall. He threw a punch, but I ducked, and his fist went through the wall. He quickly came at me again, this time backing me into a corner. I could tell by the way he swayed that he'd been drinking. I noticed a set of golf clubs nearby and quickly retrieved a nine iron. I held it up in the air, ready to swing if he attempted another attack. He held his ground.

"You're full of shit!" he slurred, his breath stinking of gin. "You know that?!"

"I know that Beth still loves you. So much so that she pretended to be Margaret just so she could be with you."

He bobbed back and forth for a few seconds and then plopped down on a rather expensive looking couch. "Why are you doing this to me? Is this some kind of twisted punishment for having an affair? That's not against the law, you know."

"No." I put down the nine iron and sat in a matching recliner across from him. "But attempted murder is."

"I didn't try to kill Beth!"

"Did you hire someone to do it? With her out of the way, you and Margaret could've finally been together."

"Once Beth found out about Maggie and me, she was going to break it off with me anyway. I didn't need to kill her to make that happen."

I read his mind. Even with an alcohol-induced, disoriented thought process, Bobby made it very clear that he had nothing to do with what happened to Beth. In fact, his brain took him back to the night the attack occurred. He was at home when he received the call and genuinely shocked to hear about it. After he found out, he called Margaret and told her they had to cool it for a while, more out of how it might appear than the fact his fiancée had been severely beaten.

I honestly couldn't see what drew Beth to him in the first place. She knew he was a liar and a cheater, yet she still had feelings for him. At that very moment, he continued to nourish his deceitful nature by plotting what he would tell the authorities if necessary as well as the senior partners when he returned to work. He planned to tell them that Margaret had become obsessed with him and threatened to hurt Beth if he didn't end the engagement. As irrational and paranoid as it was, he saw it as a way to get the heat off him completely so he could ensure his long-term place at the firm.

"So, what now?" he asked. "Am I still a suspect?"

"Not for me, you're not," I told him.

"Is Beth going to be okay?"

"I don't know. She's stable right now but that could change at any time. Is there anyone you can think of that might have wanted Beth out of the picture?"

"No," he replied despite being ready to pin the blame on Margaret if it came to it. "She didn't have any enemies if that's what you mean."

"That's what I figured. She's a good person. Most good people are well-liked...even if they're not appreciated." I stood. "Thank you for your time."

"I'll see you out." He got up and blundered over to the door. He opened it to the outside world "Hey, no hard feelings about me pouncing on you when you got here, alright? I've been under a lot of stress lately. It's not something I would've done under normal circumstances."

"Of course not." I stepped out of his apartment. As he closed the door, I felt a buzz in my pocket. I retrieved my phone and saw that I'd received a text from Linden. "This better be good," I said out loud and then read it.

Linden: Meet me at the police station ASAP.

Chapter Twenty

I took another Uber to the police station. When I arrived, there was a local news van parked right outside the station. A young reporter spoke to a woman in uniform. As I got out and approached the front door, I noticed that the woman had a name badge that said "Sheriff Luttrell." I opened the door and was about to step inside when their conversation struck me like a lightning bolt.

"Is it true that you have the Highway Killer in custody?" asked the reporter.

"You know I can't comment on that, Tom," Sheriff Luttrell told him. She caught wind of my eavesdropping and scowled at me. "Can I help you, sir?"

"I'm sorry," I said. "I'm looking for Agent Linden. He asked me to meet him here."

"You must be Mr. Crawford," she said. "Excuse me, Tom." She moved away from the reporter. "I'm Sheriff Luttrell."

I shook her hand. "Pleased to meet you."

"How about we step inside?" she suggested.

"Of course." I held the door open for her and then followed her into the station. "This is a very nice town you have here."

"Why don't we just cut the crap?" she said. "Linden says you can read minds."

"I dabble every now and then."

"Well, I don't buy into psychic mumbo jumbo. As far as I'm concerned, astrology and all that supernatural nonsense is for suckers."

"Duly noted."

"Now what we have here is—"

"Crawford," Linden said as he suddenly appeared. "Where have you been?"

"Me?" I said. "You just disappeared at the hospital."

"I'll let you take it from here," Sheriff Luttrell said to Linden and then walked away.

"She's lovely," I told Linden after she left. "Now will you tell me what this is all about?"

"Walk with me," he said and started toward the rear of the station. "Did you go anywhere after the hospital?"

"I went to see Bobby Fugate," I said as we paced side by side.

He stopped mid-step. "By yourself? Are you crazy?"

"What was I supposed to do? Sit around and do nothing? I finally got Beth retracing her steps. Did you want me to waste time and risk losing the progress I've made?"

He held up his hand annoyingly like a referee calling a time out. "Alright. Fine. Did he talk to you?"

"Yes. He didn't try to kill Beth. He cheated on her, but that's all."

"Did you read his mind to confirm?"

I nodded. "Now can we please get to back to why we're here?"

"Absolutely." He motioned to a hallway that led to another part of the station. "Right this way."

We walked down the hallway and stopped at a room at the end. He knocked on the door and a detective with a badge on his hip opened it. He let us in, and we immediately came upon a one-way mirror with a view into an adjacent room. Through the mirror, I saw an older man with shaggy hair and an unkempt beard sitting at a small table. He wore torn overalls and a dirty white t-shirt underneath.

"Who is that?" I asked.

"That's Leonard Feister," said the detective. "Who are you?"

"This is Max Crawford," answered Linden. "He's with me."

The detective nodded. "Same story," he said, motioning to Leonard. "Hasn't changed a word of it."

"What story? What does this guy have to do with anything?"

"Will you give us a minute?" Linden asked the detective.

"Sure," said the detective as he exited the room. "Gotta take a piss anyway."

"Over the past twenty years, there have been a series of unsolved murders that took place between Ohio and Kentucky," Linden explained after the detective left. "Each one involved a young woman about Beth's age."

"So, what's the connection?" I asked.

"Every one of them was beaten to death and their bodies found near a highway."

"Why didn't you tell me this earlier?"

"I wanted us to rule out other possibilities first. I wasn't sure it was even relevant."

"Relevant?! How could it not be relevant?!"

"Because the last murder took place eleven years ago. It could've been someone pretending to be the original killer to get us off track. I didn't want it to taint your investigation."

"Fine," I sighed. "Despite the fact that, once again, you've withheld vital information from me, I'm going to go along with it for Beth's sake."

"Good. So, like I said, the last murder was over a decade ago. All of a sudden, this guy…" He pointed at Leonard through the one-way mirror. "Comes into the police station and confesses to every one of the murders, including the attack on Beth."

"How many were there before Beth?"

"Five. Two of them were a few weeks apart. The other three were separated by years."

"How old is this Feister guy?"

"Sixty-six. He's lived outside of Louisville his whole life. He would've been forty-five at the time of the first murder and fully capable of committing the others."

"And I suppose you want me to read his mind to see if he's telling the truth."

He patted me on the back. "That's why I like you, Crawford. You're always a step ahead where I need you."

Ignoring his self-serving admiration, I went into the interrogation room. Leonard Feister barely even gave me a glance. I sat down in the chair across from him. Rather than speak to him immediately, I read his thoughts instead. He wondered who I was but refused to give me the satisfaction of asking. I pulled a picture of Beth from my pocket and laid it on the table in front of him. He recognized her right away, but it was the same photograph used in the newspaper.

"Why you showin' me that?" he asked. "I already told you I done it."

"What did you do exactly?"

He sighed. "I beat her up. I beat all of 'em up. She just got lucky."

"Is she lucky to be in a coma?"

"Better than bein' dead."

"I'm Max Crawford," I finally introduced myself. "I'm working with the local and federal authorities. So, you say you beat her up. How many times did you hit her?"

"I can't remember that! Look, I said what I'm gonna say to those other fellows." He crossed his arms. "You're wastin' your time."

I delved further into his mind to discover that he wanted to be famous. He fantasized about being talked about on television and having books written about him. He even imagined a movie about his life and being portrayed by Al Pacino. With all the daydreaming going on, I couldn't see if he had actually done anything wrong. I needed him to be in the moment. I pointed to the picture of Beth.

"Tell me about the night you beat her," I said.

"Jesus Christ," he muttered. "You're not gonna let up. Are you? I was driving around looking for women. I found one, and I beat her up."

I took another glimpse into his thoughts. He still wasn't focused on Beth or the others.

He was no longer fantasizing though. This time, his daily routine went through his head. He basically worked all day at a factory and then went home to be alone at night. Nothing stood out except the fact a pervasive sadness permeated his entire life. All he wanted was to be noticed. It didn't matter for what.

"Do you have a family, Leonard?" I asked.

"I got nobody," he answered.

"How does that make you feel?"

"What the hell kind of dumbass question is that?"

"Here's what I think, Leonard. I think you made the whole thing up."

"Why would I do that?"

"Because you want to be remembered for something. Even if it's bad."

"That's not true!"

"If it's not, then tell me about the night you beat her," I said, motioning to the photo of Beth a second time.

"I don't remember all the details! It was late at night!"

I saw that, as much as he tried, he couldn't recall any specifics about his alleged encounter with Beth. "You're lying, Leonard."

"I am not!"

"Then tell me one thing. What was she wearing that night?"

After imagining several different outfits, he settled on generic. "A green dress!"

"Nope." I got up from my chair. "She wore denim jeans with a blue and white University of Kentucky t-shirt." I started to leave the interrogation room. "Goodbye, Leonard."

"Wait!" he called after me pleadingly. "I can tell you about the others! I know their names! I know their birthdays! I even know the days I killed 'em and where we were!"

I read his mind again to see that he had researched the other victims online long after their murders took place. "That's all public knowledge, Leonard. We're finished here."

I rejoined Linden on the other side of the mirror. I'd never experienced someone lying about committing a crime before. However, it didn't surprise me. I'd encountered several inmates that exuded pride for what they'd done. Somehow notoriety overshadowed remorse, and they thrived on the attention it brought them. Leonard Feister was neither responsible for what happened to Beth nor the murders of the other women. He just wanted credit for it. I watched through the one-way mirror as he put his head down on the table.

"Nothing?" said Linden.

"Nope," I replied. "If he did it, there would be at least some memory of it floating around. All I found evidence of is a desperate man whose greatest fear is to be forgotten."

"That's a shame. I was hoping we had him."

"Sorry to disappoint you."

"It's not your fault. Have you made any headway with Beth?"

"Some, but she's still not remembering enough to say who did it."

"How'd you know what she was wearing the night of her attack?"

"I didn't." I motioned to Feister through the one-way mirror. "I just wanted to prove that he didn't either."

"I see. Well, let's get you back to the hospital. Anything you need from me?"

"All of the information you can get on the murder victims. If they're somehow connected to Beth, I need to know."

Before we left the police station, Linden told Sheriff Luttrell that Leonard Feister was no longer a suspect. She didn't buy it. Truthfully, it didn't make any difference to me if she thought the Easter Bunny did it. What was most important was that I got back to Beth. When we arrived at the hospital, I quietly entered her room. Allie sat by her bed reading a book to her. It reminded me of how I used to read to Katie when she was little. She noticed me and stopped.

"I'm sorry," she said, getting up from her chair. "I'll get out of your way."

"No need to apologize," I assured her. "I think it's nice. I'm sure it makes Beth feel good hearing your voice. Where is Mr. Martin?"

She frowned. "He's at home. To be honest with you, his mind isn't what it used to be. He gets…confused."

"I'm sorry to hear that." Even though I'd already noticed, there was no reason to make her feel worse by mentioning it. I motioned to Beth. "If you'd like to stay, I can come back."

"Oh, no. I'll go. I'd rather you continue your work." She went to the door. "Thank you again, Mr. Crawford."

"I haven't done enough to deserve it, but you're welcome."

She smiled. "You deserve it. The simple fact you care enough to try speaks volumes."

After she left, I sat down by Beth. I focused on her and,

without hesitation, projected into her subconscious. I materialized on the beach where I had left her during our last encounter. I saw the two chairs she had willed to appear, but she was
nowhere to be found. I scanned up and down the shoreline but
still saw no trace of her. And then I looked out at the water.
About a hundred feet from the bank, she floated on her back as
the sun's radiance shone down on her.

She appeared as peaceful as she did lying in her sterile hospital bed, only much freer.

Chapter Twenty-One

I sat down in the chair and waited for her to swim to the shore. I didn't want to interfere if the experience was giving her some sort of relief from reality. I watched as she eventually backstroked her way into shallow water and then stood up with the ocean level to her waistline.

She wore a one-piece swimsuit. She waded toward the bank and, when she finally noticed me, seemed to come out of a trance.

"Hey, there," she said as she stepped into the sand. Her body and hair instantaneously dried. "How long have you been here?"

"Not long," I answered. "I didn't want to disturb you."

She plopped down in the chair next to me. "You're not disturbing me. I know it sounds strange, but, while you were gone, I missed you." After a moment of awkward silence, she pointed to the water. "You should try it. It feels great."

"Maybe some other time. But feel free to go back in if you want."

She shook her head. "I'm okay. What did you find out while you were gone?"

"Bobby didn't have anything to do with the attack."

"I told you. He's an asshole, not a killer."

"There is one other thing that came to light. Do you know anything about the Highway Killer?"

As soon as I said the words, Beth fell out of her chair and onto the ground. Her eyes rolled into the back of her head, and she began to convulse. I hurriedly went to her side and held up her head. Her skin turned bright red, and her face started to morph into that of the crimson creature she'd become on several occasions. Wanting to act quickly, I carefully turned her head toward the ocean.

"Beth, listen to me," I spoke calmly. "You can fight this. You're still safe. You're still at the beach. Don't let this thing take over. Look out at the water."

She trembled even harder but forced her eyes back into place. Just as her whole body was transforming, she fixed her gaze on the horizon and, within a few seconds, her face shifted back to her own and her normal skin color returned. Before long, there was no trace of the creature left. She sat up and looked at me with a confused expression, as if she had no recollection of what happened.

"Did I fall or something?" she asked.

"Yes," I lied. "But you're alright now. Do you remember anything?"

"Just that you were asking me something. What was it?"

I smiled at her. "It can wait." I helped her up, and we both sat down again. "As soon as you're ready, we'll leave the beach and get back to work."

I hated that I'd added any stress, but the fact she had such a strong reaction when I mentioned the Highway Killer brought up a lot of questions. Had she encountered the individual responsible for the deaths of five other women? Or was it copycat, possibly someone like Leonard Feister except actually willing to kill for the attention? Or was her attack the act of a "thug" as Linden had initially suggested? He mentioned that her purse was missing from her car when the authorities found it. Perhaps someone intended to rob her and ended up trying to kill her out of fear of being identified. Ultimately, only she knew for sure, and I obviously had to be very careful how I solicited information from her.

"You were right," she said after gazing at the ocean a little while longer. "I really needed this."

She stood up and closed her eyes. The water, the sand, and the peaceful atmosphere changed back into the late-night road that we had escaped from during my last visit. The convertible reappeared as did the row of seemingly endless houses with the same upstairs light guiding the way. Beth got into the car and started the engine. I hopped in on the passenger's side. We drove about a fourth of a mile to the first house and then exited the vehicle.

"Are you sure you're okay?" I asked.

"I don't have much of a choice," she said. "Do I?"

We made our way to the front porch, and I was happy to see that Bobby's Bizzaro world alter-ego and his den of snakes did not make another appearance. We stepped inside the house, and Beth went ahead of me into the kitchen. I watched as she poked around, opening pantries and peeking under the table. When she seemed satisfied, she rejoined me in the entryway.

"Were you looking for the little girl?" I asked.

"Not necessarily," she replied. "Like you said, we might have missed something the last time. I want to make sure we search every cranny."

After investigating downstairs and finding nothing, we went to the second floor and started with the first unlit room. Just as before, it had a set of bunkbeds, white dresser, and doll-house-sized model of the home we were in, complete with the miniature light in the upstairs room. Beth moved around the room, lifting the mattresses on the beds and pulling drawers out of the dresser. In both cases, she came up empty. She then examined the dollhouse.

It also provided no hints as to why the life-sized version kept popping up down the road.

Once she finished, she checked the other two identical rooms. I stood in the hallway as she repeated her routine from the first room. As I expected, they were all the same down to even the minutest of details. After she finished, she directed her attention to the empty but well-lit room at the end of the hallway. We went in together and once again found the photograph of the little girl on the floor underneath the glow of the single lightbulb. She picked it up and studied it, only to shake her head.

"I don't understand," she said, handing the picture to me. "What are we missing?"

I noticed the fog surrounding the girl, a detail I would've

paid more attention to the last time had the subject in the photo not appeared downstairs in the kitchen and started throwing dishes. I looked closely and saw that there was a building behind the haze with faint, illegible letters on it. Just as with the imaginary fence surrounding the "retirement" hotel, Beth had evidently put a mental block on *where* the girl was in the picture.

"We need that to go away," I said, motioning to the dense mist.

She shrugged. "How do we do that?" she said.

"Not we. You. You need to focus on it and make it lift like you did before. There's something behind there, but only you can access it."

She took the picture from me and concentrated on the fog. After a few seconds, nothing happened. She became frustrated and almost threw the photograph to the ground. But she stopped herself and tried again. She kept her eyes transfixed on the haze until it finally began to vanish. As it slowly disappeared, the building and the words on it came into view. It said, "Thomas Frederick Elementary School." Once it was fully visible, I noticed Beth had a tear coming down her cheek.

"That's the school I went to when I was a kid," she said, wiping her face. "I still don't recognize the girl."

"Can you take us there?" I asked, pointing to the building.

She nodded and then put the photograph down on the ground in the same spot we'd originally discovered it. As we moved downstairs, I halfway expected to hear the little girl smashing dishes against the wall. But it was as dark and silent as when we first entered. We stepped outside onto the front porch and into the welcome sunlight. I immediately noticed that Thomas Frederick Elementary School had appeared directly across the street from the house.

"Wow," I marveled. "You work fast. I figured we'd have to drive there."

She shook her head. "Somehow this one came pretty easily," she said. "I guess it's because I remember it so well. I just don't know what it has to do with the attack."

We crossed the street and stopped in front of the school at the spot where the little girl's picture was taken, that is, *if* it was taken and not a figment of Beth's imagination. We waited a moment, but nothing happened. We moved to the set of double glass doors that served as the school's entrance. Beth pushed one of them open with ease and led the way inside. To our right there was a main office with a receptionist's desk and a suite of smaller offices behind it.

She pointed toward the back of the suite. "Principal Billings' office was the last on the right," she said.

"Spend a lot of time there. Did you?" I jested.

"Actually, I was a good girl. I only saw him when he gave out McDonald's coupons to students that made honor roll."

We continued down the first hall and then followed a maze deeper into the school. We came upon a set of classrooms, and Beth stopped to read the name on one of the doors. She burst into laughter. I glanced to see what name had caused such a reaction and, not surprisingly, discovered that it was none other than the infamous Miss Schneiderfelt, Beth's third-grade teacher and one-time transformative subject.

She peeked inside the room and turned on the light. "I can't believe it." She motioned toward the perfectly lined rows of desks facing a chalkboard. "It's exactly like it was when I was a kid."

"Of course, it is. It's how you remember it."

"Not everything is how I remember it. I don't seem to recall my house catching on fire or my ex-fiancé turning into a circus freak."

"It is possible that recent events have skewed your perception of things. The idea is to figure out what things and why."

Before she could respond, a shrill, Leprechaun-esque laugh echoed down the hall. Beth suddenly seemed possessed and went to a desk in the center of the classroom. She sat in it and stared vacantly at the chalkboard. A piece of white chalk levitated from the tray attached to the bottom. Like something out of a ghost story, it wrote a familiar sequence of numbers on the board. "2-6-7-21-31." The laughter continued and grew louder as if it were coming toward us.

Beth snapped out of her trance. "What is that?!" she asked.

"Don't worry," I told her. "We can handle anything that—"

Cutting me off midsentence, an old man in a custodian's uniform tackled me to the ground. He climbed on top of me and started to strangle me. He had grey hair, three-day stubble on his chin, and crooked yellow teeth with saliva dripping from his mouth. As he attempted to choke me, he continued to laugh the same high-pitched laugh. Beth came out of the room and pushed him off me. He ran straight at Beth, but she willed a plunger to appear in her hand and stuck the rubber end onto his mouth. He kept laughing, but at least it was muffled.

"Who is that?!" I asked as I got to my feet.

"It's Mr. Arnez, the school janitor!" she said, backing him against the wall with the plunger. "I've never seen him like this before!"

Mr. Arnez shrunk down to a one-foot-tall version of himself, freeing himself from the plunger's grasp, and ran off down the hall. Beth went after him and I followed close behind, wondering what the hell was happening. She chased the little janitor into a girls restroom in an adjacent hallway. He bolted into a stall and leapt on top of the toilet. He hit the flush button and, right as Beth tried to grab him, dove into the commode and went down with the flow.

She turned to me with a perplexed look on her face. "I've seen some weird shit," she said. "But *that* was some weird shit!"

"Do you think he had anything to do with—"

"No. He died when I was in fifth grade. I always thought he was a little strange. He and my dad grew up together."

"Interesting. Can I show you something?" I led her back to Miss Schneiderfelt's classroom and pointed to the numbers on the chalkboard. "Does that mean anything to you?"

She became quiet and approached the board with trepidation. "It seems familiar, but I don't know where I've seen it before."

"That pattern has come up several times in one way or another. It must mean something. Are you sure you can't remember?"

She ruminated for a moment and then shook her head. "I'm sorry, but I've got nothing."

"It's okay. Why don't we look around some more? Maybe we can find a clue."

We continued further into the school, passing other class-rooms along the way but finding nothing of any significance. When we reached the last hallway, there was a glass door at the end that led outside to a playground. Beth opened the door and smiled when she saw the conglomeration of multicolored, plastic slides and flimsy bridges. There was also a swing set and a sandbox obscured by some of the equipment.

"I used to love coming out here for recess," she reminisced. "It was one of the only times you could just be a kid and not have to worry about anything."

"I didn't particularly care for recess," I said. "Too loud. I'd rather stay in class and read a book."

She grinned. "You know, I can see that about you."

"What's that supposed to mean?"

"Nothing." She walked toward the swing set but stopped when the sandbox came into full view. "It's her," she whispered.

I quickly went to her and saw the little girl from the house building a sandcastle with varying sizes of red plastic buckets. "Does she realize we're here?" I asked.

"Of course, I do," said the girl as she carefully shaped the second level of the sandcastle. "I'm not blind."

Beth moved to the sandbox and crouched down beside her. "Are you still angry with me?"

"Nope," replied the girl. "It's not your fault."

"What's not my fault?"

The girl sighed. "What happened to us, silly."

"Us?"

The girl turned toward the playset. "You can come out now."

One by one, four other girls around the same age emerged from underneath and behind the playset. The first two wore dresses with multicolored stripes and polka dots that looked straight out of the sixties. The third one wore a green pastel knit sweater and matching skirt that would've both been in style in the late seventies. The last one wore more modern attire like our friend in the sandbox, except for a few gaudy touches that screamed nineteen eighties.

They stood in a row as if they were modeling for a retro fashion show.

The girl in the apple-patterned dress got up from the sand-box and joined them. "So..." she said to Beth. "What are you going to do now?"

Chapter Twenty-Two

The girls disappeared, and the clouds darkened. Beth immediately took shelter underneath the covered part of the play equipment that had an attached, oversized tic-tac-toe set with moveable, cylindrical pieces. Figuring she knew something I didn't, I crawled under the plastic steps leading up to one of the slides and sat next to her on the ground. It began to rain and thunder. Lightning crashed in the distance. We watched in silence as water slowly filled the sandbox.

"Pretty soon, it'll be mud and sludge," Beth said listlessly. "No one will be able to play in it."

"Do you have any idea who those girls were?" I asked, neglecting to mention the fact that there were five of them and the Highway Killer had murdered five women before Beth's attack.

She shook her head. "Do you?"

"I have an idea, but I'm not a hundred percent certain. Beth, I'm sorry, but I'm going to have to leave you again."

She turned to me, slightly alarmed. "Why? You just got back."

"I need to research something. I won't be gone long."

She stared at me intently. "You have kind eyes. Did you know that?"

"Excuse me?"

"Your eyes. There's a kindness about them. You don't see that much anymore. Most people's eyes are hollow like there's nothing behind them."

"Honestly, I don't pay attention to people's eyes. It's their brains that stick out for me."

"I bet you wish you could turn it off sometimes. Just to escape from it for a while."

"Sure, but I can't. It's always with me whether I like it or not."

"But it doesn't hurt to pretend." She reached out and put her hand on mine. "Does it?"

I withdrew my hand from hers, trying not to act as uncomfortable as I felt. "I promise. I'll be back before you know it. Will you still be here?"

She shrugged. "Maybe. Or maybe I'll be at the beach again. Or maybe I'll be in Paris."

She grinned at me. "I guess you'll just have to find me."

After I left her mind and returned to the hospital room, I hesitated to leave for a moment.

In my experience, once a subject started to seek out distractions, that was typically the time he was closest to a realization. Finding ways to avoid facing the truth tended to serve an underlying need to evade the pain that came with it. Obviously, Beth was quite different from the inmates, but, if history taught me anything, telling me I had kind eyes and touching my hand meant we were on the brink of something. I just needed to be careful getting us there.

I left her room and asked one of the nurses if she could direct me to a business center.

She frowned at me as if to say "This ain't the Four Seasons, buddy." A head nurse was kind enough to let me use her tiny space behind the receptionist's desk. I got onto the internet and did a search for "the Highway Killer." Several options popped up, and I clicked on one near the top that said, "Victims Over Time."

At the top of the webpage, a newspaper article from 2008, there were five pictures of women that appeared to be in their middle to late twenties. I thought about Leonard Feister for a moment and wondered if he had looked at the same site before he fabricated his story about being the killer. I read through the piece to discover that three of the victims lived in Louisville and the other two lived in small towns in Ohio. Every one of them was, as Linden lately explained, beaten to death and left in a field off a highway.

I further investigated to learn that the first victim, Mary Madsen, was killed in 1989, which would've placed her in the late sixties as a young child. The next one, Linda Kassi, was murdered two weeks later, indicating a similar time frame for when she was a little girl. The third woman, Ashley Rogers, was found near the Ohio River in March of 1996, making her a child of the seventies. The last two, Macie Lox and Rhonda Sinclair, were killed two years apart in 2006 and 2008. They also both attended "Thomas Frederick Elementary School" in the 1980s, ten years before Beth would attend there for her first year as a kindergartener.

I looked at the photos of the five women again and pictured the five little girls at Beth's imaginary playground standing in a row above them. The timeline fit perfectly. Not only that but, on some level, Beth knew them. Whether she had researched them or was somehow connected to them remained to be seen. Whatever the case, it couldn't have been a coincidence, especially since she'd had such a strong reaction when I mentioned the Highway Killer on the beach.

Just then my cell phone buzzed. It was Jessica. "Hello?" I answered.

"Hey, stranger," she said. "It seems like years since I've talked to you."

"Yeah, sorry. I've been so caught up in this case, I've—"

"You don't have to explain. So, what is she like?"

"Who?"

She laughed. "The woman in the coma, you goofball. What is she like?"

"She's, uh, a nice person, I suppose."

"That's it? Nice?"

"I don't know, Jess. She's been through a lot. I haven't exactly gotten to know her on a personal level."

"Then how have you gotten to know her? I'm sorry. I just miss you. That's all. You know how I get when you're gone."

"I know, but I'll be home before you know it. I really think we're getting closer to finding some answers."

"That's great. I love you. I won't pester you anymore."

"You're not pestering me. There's just a lot going on."

"I'll let you go then. Call me when you can."

Once when I was six years old, my mom baked an apple pie. When it was it ready, she took it out of the oven and placed it on the counter to cool off before dinner. She left to go to the store, leaving my dad and me alone at the house. While my dad was busy watching TV, I sat in the kitchen, tortured by the enticing aroma of the pie as it sat on the counter. Unable to take it any longer, I took a bite and then haphazardly spread it around to look like I hadn't. When my mother got home, all she said was hello to me and I immediately confessed. Why? Because women have an uncanny way of making me feel like they already know.

"She kissed me," I told Jessica.

"What?!"

"One of the first times I went into her mind, I pretended to be her fiancé and she kissed me, thinking I was him."

"Why the hell would you do that?!"

"I was trying to trigger her memory."

"Well, it sounds like you triggered something else!"

"Look, I just thought I should tell you. As soon as she did it, I pulled away."

"Jesus, Max. Anything *else* like that happen?"

"Um…she may have told me I had kind eyes and touched my hand. But that's it. I swear."

"Does this woman have feelings for you?"

"Of course not!" I insisted. "She's been traumatized. Any interest in me is purely an avoidance mechanism. If I were her, I wouldn't want to relive what happened. I'm sure that when I go back, she'll have realized she has to or else we'll never know who attacked her."

"If you say so."

"Trust me. It was only a momentary lapse of reason. I'm certain she's forgotten about it."

She sighed. "Just solve the case and come home. We need you here too."

"How's Katie?"

"She's okay. I think your little pep talk helped."

"Good. I love you, Jess. Always and forever."

"I love you too, Max. I'll talk to you later."

After I got off the phone, I realized that the receptionist had been eavesdropping. She hurriedly opened a medical chart on her desk and pretended to scan through it. I left the head nurse's office space and walked back toward Beth's room. Along the way, I ran into Linden, who was watching a soap opera in the waiting room. It was so out of character for him that I nearly laughed. After reporting my findings to him, I quietly entered Beth's room and sat down by her side. I focused on her face and projected into her mind.

When I materialized inside, I was standing in a fancy restaurant. The waiter from the "retirement" hotel passed me holding a tray with a bottle of champagne and two glasses on it. I walked into the main dining area and saw several tables, all of which were candle lit and decorated with long stemmed roses. A couple sat at each table, some of them talking and holding hands. The familiar waiter sat the bottle of champagne down on a table where only one person sat across from an empty chair. It was Beth. She was wearing a long white dress and makeup.

Her hair looked like she had spent the day at a salon. She saw me, and a violinist appeared beside her and began to play soft, romantic music.

"There you are," she said, smiling and waving me toward her. "I was afraid I was going to have to eat alone."

"Aw, shit," I said to myself.

Chapter Twenty-Three

I walked over to the table and sat across from her, knowing full well that I had to be careful about what I said and how I acted. I had some experience with inmates trying to befriend me in dreams so I could enable them but none in the realm of romantic transference. I suppose I should consider it a blessing given the fact I worked in a prison. Nevertheless, I was treading into new territory.

"It's good to see you," she said, still smiling.

"You as well," I said.

She looked around and sighed. "Bobby never took me to a place like this. I was lucky if I got Chinese takeout on a Saturday night."

"You deserve better." I knew it was a leading statement but couldn't stop the part of myself that needed to console. I immediately went to the follow-up. "I'm sure there's someone out there for you. Maybe you just haven't met them yet."

"Or maybe I have."

"Have I showed you a picture of my wife and kids?" I dug into my pocket and willed a photograph of Jessica and Katie to appear in my hand. I took it out and held it out for her to see. "Aren't they something?"

She waved it away, refusing to look. "If they're so special, why aren't you with them instead of me?"

"Because I'm here to help you."

"You want to help me?" She snapped her fingers and a slow ballad played overhead. "Dance with me."

I shook my head. "I don't think that's a good idea."

"Why not?"

"Because I'm married."

"Jesus, Max. I asked you to dance, not take your pants off."

"Look, Beth. You're a great person…" I motioned all around us. "But this is just a distraction. I really think we're getting closer to—"

"Blah. Blah. Blah. Aren't you getting tired of talking about the same thing over and over again? I know I am."

"I know this must be hard for you."

She turned red and picked up an imaginary fork off the table. "I swear to God if you say one more thing like that, I'm going to stab my eye out with this fork."

I held up my hands in surrender. "Okay. You're obviously not ready."

She placed the fork down on the table and suddenly became pleasant again. "Listen, I really do appreciate what you're trying to do. That's one of the reasons I like you so much. Tell you what. One dance and we'll go right back to the boring business of finding out who tried to kill me. Deal?"

"Beth, please."

She sat back in her chair and crossed her arms, unwilling to budge. Making it even more awkward, she reminded me of Katie in the middle of one of her stubborn teenager mutinies. I found that the only way to get her out of it was to compromise somehow while still getting her to see why her behavior is unacceptable and childish. In Beth's case, however, all the cards were in her hands.

"Okay," I finally said. "One harmless, little dance. But after that, we get back to work. Do I have your word?"

She held up her hand, palm out. "Girl scout's honor," she said.

She got up and moved to an open area between tables. All the other lights in the imaginary restaurant dimmed, and a spotlight fell exclusively on her. The other patrons turned their full attention to her as if she were a bride about to have her first dance. She motioned me toward her. I sighed and left the comfort of my chair. I joined her on the floor, and she put her arms around my neck. I hesitantly put mine around her waist, careful to not let my hands fall too low.

I'd always hated dances. When I was in junior high, a friend of mine talked me into going to one. It was in the eighties so the music they played was either hit or miss although usually the latter. I remember hiding behind the punch bowl until a determined eighth grade girl approached me and asked me to dance. Sweating, I walked out to the floor with her and proceeded to make a fool of myself. I continued my uncoordinated streak with Beth as I accidently stepped on her foot.

"Sorry," I said.

"It's okay," she said, her face a little too close to mine. "Do you remember when we kissed on the veranda?"

"Uh, actually you kissed me because you thought I was Mr. Stevens."

She giggled. "Ah, yes. Mr. and Mrs. Stevens. We could always pretend to be them again and see where things take us."

I let go of her. "Beth."

"Alright, fine," she said, coaxing me back into our dancing position. "My point was the kiss was nice, no matter who you were pretending to be."

We danced a while longer. She eventually put her head on my shoulder, but I kept my hands in the same platonic spot. At one point, I convinced myself I was dancing with my grandmother to preclude even the remotest of inclinations. When the song finally came to an end, I took a deep breath and exhaled. I released my hold on Beth and started to remind her of her promise. Before I could get out the words, she sprung at me and abruptly kissed me on the lips. I instantly pulled away from her.

"Wow," she said facetiously. "I must really be disgusting."

"It's not that and you know it."

"Then what's the problem?"

"I already told you. I have a family."

"But what if you didn't? Then would you?"

I shook my head. "It's not ethical."

"Screw ethical." She paused for a moment and glanced at the imaginary patrons gawking at us from their tables. "Oh, I get it. You want us to go someplace more private?"

"I didn't say that. I—"

She snapped her fingers, and the restaurant promptly

changed into the beach. We were at the same spot as last time except it was nighttime and the full moon provided the only illumination. In lieu of the two chairs from before, there was a blanket spread out on the sand with a bottle of wine in an alloy chiller and two glasses beside it. I was taken aback at how quickly she transformed the surroundings. Whereas earlier it was a gradual process, now it was the equivalent of flipping a light switch.

"Impressed?" she said.

"I see you've been practicing," I said.

She moved closer to me and lifted her dress over her head. "Well, I had a good teacher." She let it fall to the ground.

"What are you doing?"

"This is my mind and I can do what I want in it." She proceeded to take off her shoes. "Right now, I feel like being naked."

"This isn't going to change anything."

After removing her shoes, she reached around to unhook her bra. "We'll see about that."

Right as she began to remove the undergarment, I shifted one hundred and eighty degrees. "I'm not playing this game with you."

"Then let's play a different one." She threw her bra onto the sand by my feet, followed seconds later by her panties. "Turn around."

"Beth—"

"Do it or you're not welcome in my head anymore."

I slowly turned to face her, all the while averting my eyes. "Are you happy?"

"Now take off your clothes."

"I'm not doing that."

"Fine. I'll do it for you." She snapped her fingers.

I looked down to see that I was nude but in another man's body. "Are you kidding?" I pointed at the freakishly large penis she'd conjured between my legs. "That's not even mine!"

She reached out to touch my face. "Then show me."

I withdrew from her and willed myself to be dressed again. "That's enough."

"Aren't you attracted to me?"

"Do you want to know the truth?"

"Yes."

"Alright. When I see you, I see my daughter. I think about how much I want to protect her from the world and that makes me want to help you even more."

She shook her head in disbelief. "You're an asshole. You know that?" She stormed off down the beach.

"Beth, wait."

"Just leave me alone!"

"I was being honest!"

"Go away, Max! I don't want you here!"

Still in the buff, Beth disappeared along the shoreline. Not wanting to be where I wasn't welcome, I disconnected from her mind. No sooner than I had returned to the hospital room, a nurse entered and went straight to Beth's vital sign machines. Once my head cleared a little, I saw that her heart rate was slightly elevated. I got up before the nurse could ask me to leave and stepped out into the hallway to find Linden waiting for me.

"What'd you do this time, Crawford?"

I shook my head and walked past him. "Told the truth," I replied.

"Couldn't you at least sugar-coat it a little?"

Ignoring him, I went into the waiting area and sat down in one of the chairs. I shut my eyes, trying to refocus and plan my next move. I had barely had a minute when my phone started buzzing in my pocket. Just knowing that it was Jessica and she was going to drill me about Beth, I took my phone out and prepared myself to tell her everything. To my surprise, however, Jessica's number didn't show up on the display screen. In its place was a local number that I didn't recognize.

Thinking it was a telemarketer, I dismissed the call and put the phone back into my pocket. Linden walked in and handed me a cup of coffee. Without saying a word, he sat across from me. I think he could tell I was spent so he left me alone and turned his attention to the telenovela on the TV. My phone buzzed again. I retrieved it from my pocket and saw that it was the same number. Linden turned his attention away from the boob tube and looked at me curiously. This time, I answered.

"Hello?" I said.

"Mr. Crawford," a sobbing voice came through the line.

"Yes?"

"It's Allie Martin, Beth's mother." She tried to compose herself. "I'm sorry to call you like this, but you were the first person that came to mind."

"It's no trouble at all. What's wrong, Mrs. Martin?"

"It's Edward." She paused for a moment. "He's missing."

Chapter Twenty-Four

I debriefed Linden on the situation, and we headed to the Martin house. I hated leaving Beth, but something told me it would be a while before she'd speak to me again. In retrospect, maybe I shouldn't have been as honest as I was with her. At least not in that moment.

Oh, well. The past is an unchangeable beast that looms like a thundercloud, and an umbrella is forever out of reach.

When we arrived at Beth's childhood home, Mrs. Martin met us on the front porch. She wasn't as put together as the first time we visited, understandably, but welcomed us with the same cordiality as before. When we entered the house, there was even a silver tray with an empty pitcher and two glasses on it neatly placed in the middle of the coffee table. She noticed the pitcher, let out a sigh, and picked it up.

"What is wrong with me?" she said. "I could've sworn I already filled this." She started for the kitchen. "I'll be right back with some fresh lemonade."

"That's not necessary, Mrs. Martin," I told her. "Don't feel like you have to cater to us. We just want to help you find your husband."

She nodded and sat down on the couch by the coffee table. "Thank you." She placed the empty pitcher back on the tray. "I appreciate you both coming so quickly."

"When was the last time you saw Mr. Martin?" asked Linden.

"Well, he said he was going to drive to town to get some supplies. There's only one place he ever goes. He's normally only gone an hour or so. After a few hours, I started to worry, so I called the store. They hadn't seen him." She began to sob. "I shouldn't have let him drive on his own. He's getting too... absent minded."

I sat by her on the couch. "We'll find him," I told her. "Do you know the way he usually goes to the get to the store?"

"Yes. It's just along the highway."

"Okay. Agent Linden and I will go and retrace his path."

"Can I come with you, please? I can't bear staying here and waiting."

"Of course, you can. As soon as you're ready, we'll all go together."

Shortly thereafter, the three of us climbed into Linden's car and followed Edward's trail. Along the way, Allie explained how things had gotten worse. Evidently, Edward had even gone so far as to stand in the middle of a room, hold an item, and completely forgot how it ended up in his hand or where he was going with it. I asked if he'd been diagnosed with anything specific and, irritated, she said he refused to see a doctor.

After driving along the highway toward Louisville for about thirty minutes, Allie spotted Edward's truck parked on the rocky shoulder near an open grass field. Linden pulled up behind the truck, and we all got out of the car. We peeked in through the windows of the truck, but he was nowhere to be found. My first thought was that he'd run out of gas and started walking toward the nearest station. However, that was quickly disproven.

"I see him!" exclaimed Allie as she looked out across the grass field and saw him wondering aimlessly in the distance. She hurried toward him, leaving Linden and me by the truck. "Edward!"

"What a shame," I said to Linden.

"You don't know the half of it," he said. "This is where they found Beth."

We walked through the field and caught up with them. Allie looked at us pleadingly. Edward, on the other hand, didn't seem to even notice any of us. He was walking around in a circle and pulling up weeds along the way. Once he had a handful, he'd toss them to the side. He continued to do so and didn't stop until he'd completed a three-hundred-and-sixty-degree rotation. He finally seemed to realize we were there.

"We can't plant anything here," he said to no one in particular. "This land is too coarse for crops."

Allie moved closer to him. "What are you talking about?" she asked. "This land isn't even yours."

He didn't acknowledge her. "A little tilling ought to loosen it up." He went toward his truck. "I just need my plow."

Linden blocked his way. "Maybe you should come with us, Mr. Martin," he said.

Edward backed away from Linden. "I know who you are. You've come to take my farm. Well, I ain't gonna let you."

Allie wept. "They're here to help, Edward," she said. "Don't you even recognize me?"

He finally looked directly at her. "Of course, I do. You're the lady from the post office."

Allie put her hand over her mouth. "I'm sorry. I can't do this right now." She walked over to the car and stood beside it, still crying.

"Guess I'm not gettin' my mail today," said Edward obliviously.

"Mr. Martin..." I began, choosing my words carefully. "I think it'd be best if you came with us."

"You boys gonna help me get my plow?"

"Sure," I replied. I felt Linden's puzzled gaze upon me but ignored it. Obviously, I didn't like deceiving Edward but didn't think he'd agree to go if I flat out told him were taking him to the hospital. "We can help you."

"Good," he said and made another attempt for his truck. "I'll drive."

I stood in his path that time since there was no way we could let him drive and risk harming himself or someone else. "How about you let me drive?" I suggested. "I know a short cut."

Edward shrugged. "Fine. As long as we get back before dark. Ain't no use workin' without daylight."

The three of us joined Allie on the side of the road by the vehicles. At that point, she was inconsolable. Unable to bear having her husband not know who she was, she elected to ride with Linden in his car while Edward and I followed in the truck. As strange as it felt driving an old pickup in rural Kentucky, it didn't compare to what came out of Edward's mouth on the way to the hospital.

"There's a bad storm comin'," he said, pointing to the clear blue sky as we rode along the highway. "Look a yonder."

"It looks okay to me, Mr. Martin," I said.

"It's not what you can see. It's what you can't see. It's like Lucifer gatherin' eggs for the harvest."

"I don't think I follow you."

He stopped talking and resigned himself to stare vacantly out the passenger's window.

I felt bad for him and his wife. First, their only daughter is attacked and put into a coma. Next, one of them loses his mind leaving the other one by herself to deal with all of it. When we arrived at the hospital, we were directed to a ward not far from Beth's. Edward went through several evaluations and, despite his protests, was admitted within an hour. After a nurse took him to his room, Allie seemed more lost than ever.

"Can we drive you home, Mrs. Martin?" I asked.

She shook her head. "I'd like to go sit with my daughter for a while," she said.

"Unless you're going to—"

"It can wait. You go ahead."

"So, what happened the last time you were in Beth's head?" Linden asked after Allie left.

"It's complicated. Just know that I now believe there's some connection to the Highway Killer. I'm just not sure what it is yet."

He nodded. "Well, it's all up to you now, Max. We don't have any suspects or clues in the real world, so the answer must be in her mind. It's time to excavate it."

Even though he used an unsettling mining metaphor in reference to Beth's brain, Linden had a point. I either had to push Beth a little more or risk the memory of the attack getting shoved further back into her unconscious. That was if she would even talk to me after I foolishly mentioned my teenage daughter when she was trying to seduce me in her birthday suit. I planned to apologize for my poor timing.

When I got to her room, I waited outside to give Allie some time alone with her. I peeked through the window to see that she was reading to her again. I hoped that, whatever the story, it was somehow giving them both some escape from their realities. After she read for a while, she placed the book down on the bedside table and got up from the chair. She stepped outside into the hallway and forced a smile when she saw me.

"Thank you," she said meekly.

"You don't need to thank me for anything, Mrs. Martin," I told her. "I saw you reading to her through the window. I hope you don't mind."

"Not at all. It's nice to know that you're watching over her. Can you do one more thing for me?"

"Of course."

"When you see her, tell her it's time to wake up."

Chapter Twenty-Five

When I entered Beth's mind, I found myself standing on the same beach as before, only this time in the middle of the day. The sun hung overhead and bore down on the sand beside my feet. I felt its warmth even though I knew it wasn't real. It's funny how the brain plays tricks on a person. It can make you feel like you're experiencing the inauthentic as easily as it can make an actual event routine and emotionless.

I saw Beth sitting near the shoreline. Luckily, she was at least wearing her one-piece swimsuit. I walked over to her, and she looked up at me. Her hair and suit were completely dry, but tiny drops of water covered her arms and legs. Yet again, the mind had its own agenda. In this case, it chose what part of reality it wanted to carry over into the unconscious and which part it wanted to discard.

"I come in peace," I told her.

She motioned to the ground beside her. "Sit down," she said. "I want to tell you something."

I did as she requested. "What is it?"

She sighed. "I want to apologize to you."

"There's no need."

"Yes, there is. I acted way out of line. You were just trying to help me, and I made a complete fool of myself."

"Well, I could've definitely handled it better."

"You handled it fine. I shouldn't have called you an 'asshole' either. You've been nothing but kind to me. I think I'm just scared."

"Of what?"

"The truth."

"About the attack?"

She nodded. "But not just that. The truth about my engagement. The truth about my condition. The universe has a way of changing everything at once and we don't get a say in the matter."

"Well, unfortunately, a lot of things are out of our control. I find that it makes the most sense to focus on the things we can. I spoke to your mom before I came back." I decided, under the circumstances, to not mention the fact her dad had been admitted to the same hospital. "She's been reading to you every time she visits."

She smiled. "She used to read to me when I was kid. She said it was to help calm me down. Honestly, I think it was as much for her as it was for me. Did she say anything about me?"

"She wants you to wake up."

"If only it were that easy." She stood up and brushed the imaginary sand off her backside. "Where do we need to go now? Back to the elementary school or the house with the light in the upstairs room?"

I stood up beside her. "I think that, when you're ready, we need to revisit the night you were attacked."

"I told you. I can't remember that night."

"Maybe there's something that could help trigger your memory."

"Like what?"

"The days leading up to it. How far back can you remember?"

She thought for a moment. "I remember going to work. I'm not sure what day, but I know we had a meeting."

"Take us there."

She concentrated, and our surroundings quickly transformed into the inside of an art gallery. We were standing among several paintings and a few sculptures, one of which depicted a monkey flying an airplane with the phrase "The Future Is Yours" carved across one of the wings. Beth moved toward one of the paintings. It was of a young woman standing near the ocean and looking out at the water.

"I don't remember that one," she said.

"Your unconscious may have created it," I said. "Let's try to keep it as close to reality as we can."

Just then a man with six arms and a third eye in his forehead walked into the room. He danced around the room, occasionally belching and emitting a green dust from his mouth. A gorilla stormed in and tackled the man to the ground. The animal ripped a hole in the man's chest and confetti shot out of his insides and into the air. The gorilla laughed and clapped its hands.

Then they both disappeared.

I looked at Beth. "Or not?" I said.

"Sorry," she said. "It's a lot of pressure."

"Well, now that you got that out of your system, where was the meeting you mentioned?"

"In our conference room. Follow me."

She led me through the gallery to a set of offices in a separate hallway. Along the way, I noticed a security guard standing near an unusual and particularly ornate work of art. It looked like life-sized origami but with crystals set into various points of its structure. In its center, there was a glowing blue orb. The security guard nodded to me as we passed him and entered the office suite.

"That's one of our most expensive pieces," Beth explained. "It's by an artist from Paraguay. It's worth seventy thousand dollars."

Before I could comment, a woman wearing a gaudy, yellow blouse accosted us. "Oh my God, Beth!" she said. "Where have you been?!" She grabbed Beth by the arm and took her away from me. "They've been waiting for you!"

Beth turned to me and shrugged as she was dragged toward a conference room in the middle of two individual offices. I stayed close behind. The woman in the awful blouse opened the door to reveal a group of half a dozen formally dressed people sitting at a long table. They turned to face Beth as she was practically shoved into the room. I slipped in after her and the woman in the shameless attire shut the door behind her. Another woman in a slightly more tasteful, brown pantsuit at the end of the table frowned at Beth.

"We thought you'd never show up," she said. "Do you have the proposal ready?"

Beth fidgeted. "Almost," she said. "I mean, I've got a couple of tweaks to make, but it should be done by Friday at the latest."

The woman sighed. "I'm afraid that won't do, Elizabeth. I called this meeting today solely for this purpose. Now present your proposal or face the consequences."

Beth twirled her hair. "I guess I'll just have to face the consequences then. What are they exactly?"

The woman laughed. "It's quite simple. We're going to suck every last drop of blood from your nubile, young body."

As it turned out, the six-armed freak and the confetti hungry primate wouldn't be Beth's only diversion from reality. The woman opened her mouth and fangs shot out from her top teeth.

The others also sprouted fangs. An older gentleman in a suit grabbed hold of Beth and threw her on top of the table. They started ripping at her clothes, one of them trying to tear off her shirt while another tugged at her pants.

She looked at me and forced a smile. "A little help?"

I sighed and willed a wooden stake to appear in my hand. I stabbed one of the vampire-art aficionados through his heart. He exploded into a patch of red pixie dust that rained down onto the floor. The rest turned their attention away from Beth and toward me. Two came at me furiously. I stabbed one of them, but the other sank his teeth into my arm. I didn't even react. I just impaled him too. They both turned into magic sprinkles like the first one.

Beth freed herself from the others and willed a stake of her own. Together, we fought off two of the remaining three and skewered them both. The woman who initially chastised Beth was the last one. She leapt on Beth's back and screeched like a wild banshee. I hurriedly speared her from behind, and she exploded all over Beth. The ground was now covered with the enigmatic, mystical powder.

"Nubile, young body?" I teased her.

"Leave me alone," she said, brushing off pixie dust. "I read a lot of vampire books as a teenager."

"Evidently fairy tales as well. So, what actually happened at the meeting?"

"They gave me an extension, but they were really snarky about it."

"I see. So, what'd you do afterwards?"

"I went home to my apartment."

"Take us there."

She nodded and, seconds later, we were standing in the living room of her apartment.

A few classic paintings decorated the walls. "Starry Night" by Vincent Van Gogh and "Persistence of Time" by Salvador Dali occupied spots perpendicular to a Monet and a framed piece I hadn't encountered before. I moved closer to it to see that it was a painting of a young woman sitting on a city bus while other shadowy, faceless figures filled seats around her. She seemed sad as she stared out of the window.

"I like this one," I told Beth. "Is it real?"

"Of course, it's real," she said, plopping down on the couch. "I painted it."

"Really? How long ago did you do this?"

"About six years ago."

"Any others?"

She shook her head. "Not since that one. I guess I just gave it up."

"That's a shame. You're very talented." I noticed a tan leather suitcase by the door and motioned to it. "Were you going somewhere?"

She stared at the luggage curiously. "I don't think so."

Even though I knew she went to her parents' house that weekend, I needed her to make her own connections. "So, what did you do when you got home?"

She sighed. "Well, I was pretty frustrated about the meeting, so I..." She saw her cell phone lying on the coffee table. "Called Bobby to vent."

"Go ahead and call him."

"Are you serious?"

"Yeah. Maybe something in your conversation sparked what happened next."

She laughed. "Alright." She picked up the phone and dialed a number. She waited.

"He's not answering."

"Did he answer that day?"

"I don't know. Wait. It's his voicemail. Jesus, I hate that voicemail." She ended the call and threw the phone onto the coffee table. "Now I remember. I left a message, but he didn't call me back."

"So, what'd you do next?"

"Let me think." She ruminated. "I wanted to get out of the city...so I decided to visit my parents."

"Thus, the suitcase."

"That's strange. Why was it already by the door when I hadn't remembered going yet?"

"Sometimes the mind leaves clues without us realizing it. We need to be on the lookout for others. They could be helpful."

Beth's baggage wasn't my first encounter with an object popping up inexplicably. An inmate I worked with by the name of Stuart Lansinger provided that experience for me.

Convicted for the first-degree murder of his girlfriend, Stacey, Stuart consistently denied any wrongdoing. Stacey worked at the pastry shop that Stuart owned and cheated on Stuart with Tommy, the young, handsome man that worked the counter.

When Stuart learned of the affair, he became angry and Stacey disappeared two days later. The remains of her mutilated body were found in an apartment complex trash bin by a couple of garbage men. All signs pointed back to Stuart, who had no alibi and, in his state of rage, carelessly left his DNA all over poor Stacey. He had been in prison a year before he agreed to work with me.

My dream visits to Stuart's subconscious took place either at the pastry shop, at his home, or in transit between the two. For a while, he tried to convince me of his innocence. And then the body parts started showing up. A severed leg suddenly appeared on his living room couch. An unattached arm fell from the sky and hit his windshield as he was driving us along an imaginary road. The pinnacle came, however, when Stacey's decapitated head appeared on display at the pastry shop between a plate of raspberry kolaches and a basket of blueberry muffins. Unable to stop the pieces of Stacey from appearing, Stuart inevitably broke down, admitted to the murder, and started the long road to rehabilitation.

"So, do we go to my parents' house now?" asked Beth.

"Let's not go straight there," I replied. "I'd like to see if anything significant occurred on your way."

"How do we do that?"

"We start driving."

We went downstairs and to her car. I thought about the convertible we rode around in before compared to her compact, economy four-seater. As nice as the previous vehicle was, it was important to relive the events leading her to attack as close to how they really happened as possible. We drove away from the apartment complex and onto the interstate. So far, nothing seemed out of the ordinary.

"Is there anything in particular you're looking for?" she asked.

"No. We won't really know what it is until we see it."

"Of course." She looked down at her gas gauge to see that it was close to empty. "Damnit. I'm almost out of gas. Wait. I can just refill it with my mind."

"Not if you stopped for gas in reality. We need to follow your path exactly as—"

"Okay. Okay. I don't see how this is supposed to help. I've made this drive dozens of times. I'm sure nothing interesting happened."

She took the first exit off the interstate and stopped at a gas station. She got out of the car and retrieved a fuel dispenser. She placed the nozzle in the filling inlet and set the hose to flow independently. She peeked in through the open door at me and shrugged. An old pickup truck pulled up to the pump next to ours. A man in his middle to late sixties got out of the truck holding a map. He wore a fuzzy flannel shirt and blue jeans with holes in them.

"Excuse me, young lady," he addressed Beth. "Do you know how I get to Highway 42?"

"Well, if you keep heading north, you'll run right into it." She walked over and pointed to the map. "See. This is I-75.

Forty-two runs parallel but intersects..." She pressed her finger on a specific spot. "Here."

"I'll be durned."

"You should get a GPS."

"Oh, no. I'm not much for technology. So where are you headed?"

"To my folks' house for the weekend."

"They live off of Forty-two?"

"No. South off of I-65 just outside of Columbia."

"Well, they're lucky to have such a friendly and helpful daughter." He smiled at her. "You have a safe trip now."

Beth smiled back at him and walked to the car. She nonchalantly removed the nozzle from the inlet and returned it to the holder. She got in the car, started it, and was about to drive away when she saw my face. I believe my expression was a mixture of total disbelief and immobilizing shock. I tried to hide it, but once my jaw fell, there was no pulling it up again. She didn't seem to understand why I would have such a reaction.

"What is it?" she asked.

I finally broke out of my paralysis. "Seriously?!" I said. "You just told a man you've never met before exactly where you're going! Did that actually happen?"

"I don't know. So, what if it did?"

"Really? Didn't your parents ever teach you about 'stranger danger'?"

"I grew up in a small town, Max. Everybody knew everybody." She started driving. "Besides, he was harmless."

"You don't know that!"

She got back on the interstate. "Trust me. I think I'd remember if some old man beat me senseless."

"Not necessarily!"

My thoughts went back to Leonard Feister, who, despite fabricating the whole story, fit the age range for someone who could've matched the timeframe between the first murder and Beth's attack. I didn't tell her that though. Even though it wasn't real, I couldn't risk her turning into the crimson creature again and veering off the road head-on into a semi. Not only would it cause a setback, but I wasn't particularly keen on even pretending to crash on the highway.

"Look, all I'm saying is it wouldn't hurt to be more careful," I told her. "The world's a dangerous place. Not everyone can be trusted."

"You see, that's exactly the kind of attitude I want to avoid. I want to believe that most people are inherently good and not develop some unhealthy paranoia just because there are a few psychos out there."

"There are definitely more than a few."

"It doesn't matter how many. I refuse to be controlled by fear."

There was no way I would tell her, but she reminded me of Katie again. I remembered taking her to kindergarten and walking her to the front door every day. And then one day she asked if I would drop her off so she could walk herself. For some reason, the idea scared the hell out of me, but I let her. She got out of the car and started toward the school. She turned and looked back at me to see if I was still there and then continued. She tripped and fell on her knees, but I let her get up on her own. She looked back once more and then went inside. It's a frightening feeling when your child goes out into the world alone.

"There's no use arguing about this," I said, realizing I was sounding too parental. "You're an adult. You're entitled to make your own decisions."

"Thank you," she said.

"So, has anything triggered a memory yet?"

"Including the old man at the gas station?" she jested.

"Definitely."

"Nope. It's all still a big blur."

We continued driving until we were out of the city and entered rural Kentucky. She took the same route Linden and I did going back and forth from the farmhouse to the hospital. I wondered how Edward was doing. I still wasn't ready to tell Beth about him, especially since we were getting so close to the night of the attack. Everything was going fine until we turned down a two-lane highway between two fields. Beth's hands trembled. She pulled off on the side of the road and put the car in park just as the rest of her body began to shake violently.

"Beth?" I said. I reached toward her but was met with a static electrical barrier. It felt like the one surrounding the "retirement" hotel except it was invisible. "You have to try to calm yourself down."

"I can't," she said. Her face started to morph into pixilated fuzziness. "I don't understand what's—"

Before she could finish, her mouth, nose, and eyes disappeared and merged with a random pattern of tiny dots that swirled around beneath her hair and above her neck. Still vibrating fiercely, she put her fingers to where her lips used to be in attempt to stop whatever was happening to her. Her hands were sucked into the whirling insanity that had become her face. Her arms followed, and she let out a muffled, metallic scream.

Not knowing what to do, I leapt toward her but bounced backward off the transparent force field and slammed against the car door. I watched in horror as the rest of her body inverted itself and got pulled into the inexplicable vortex. Her feet were the last to go inside. Once they were gone, the matrix broke up into a thousand pieces and then vanished completely. Beth had departed.

Not knowing what to do, I got out of the vehicle and began searching for her. I looked underneath the car and in the trunk. I walked out into the field on the side of the road where she had stopped, calling for her along the way. After a few minutes, I felt like I'd been there before.

And then I found her and realized why. Lying in the tall grass, bruised and bleeding, Beth was where they discovered her the morning after the attack. Her eyes slowly opened into tiny slits, and she saw me standing above her.

"Max?" she said weakly.

Chapter Twenty-Six

"Can you move?" I asked.

"I don't think so," answered Beth. "I feel kind of stuck."

"Alright, listen. I need you to tell yourself this isn't real. I need you to stand up and walk with me to the car."

She grunted, but her body stayed still. "I can't."

"Yes, you can."

"No." A tear ran down her cheek. "I'm paralyzed."

"It's all psychological. You opened your eyes. Now just lift one finger for me."

"It's not working. Please, help me."

"Maybe if we get away from here, you'll snap out of it. I'm going to pick you up. Okay?"

"Okay."

I put my hands underneath her and lifted her up into my arms. She weighed less than a feather. I carried her over to the car and, still holding her with one arm, opened the back door with my free hand. I set her down gently, letting her lie across the back seat. Her body looked tense as if had been restrained by invisible rope. I went around to the front of the car and got in on the driver's side.

"How'd you get so strong?" she asked, her voice muffled.

I smiled and started the car. "It's just a trick I picked up over the years," I explained. "I can manipulate weight with my mind."

In actuality, I learned the skill out of necessity. An inmate named Arthur Casey didn't particularly like the idea of me going into his dreams so he'd try to force me out of them.

More specifically, he had worked in construction and came at me with a wrecking ball as soon as I entered his mind. At first, I retreated, but then reminded myself that the rules of gravity didn't apply. I walked right up to him, and he swung the ball straight at me. I lifted my hand and stopped it with my pinky finger. After that, he must've thought I was some kind of wizard because he ceased the defensive strikes and cooperated.

"I'm going to your parents' house," I told her. "All I need you to do is tell yourself this isn't real."

"This…isn't…real," she said and then became quiet.

I drove along the highway until we arrived at the farm road that led to her childhood home. As I turned at the intersection, two zebras raced past, nearly sideswiping the car. I hit the brakes as two elephants thundered by in front of us, followed by two lions and two horses. I sat and watched behind the wheel as more animals ran down the highway in pairs. Hundreds of them hurried off in the opposite direction of where we were headed.

"I take it you went to Sunday School when you were a kid," I said.

"Yeah," she said sleepily. "Why?"

"The passengers of Noah's Ark just bolted."

I continued down the farm road and, apropos for the Old Testament motif, it began to rain. The closer I got to the farm-house, the harder it came down. By the time I reached the Martins' home it was pouring. I stopped the car as close to the front porch as I could. I considered willing the rain to stop but remembered that manipulating someone's mind can cause a backlash. If Beth needed it to storm, so be it.

I quickly got out of the car and went around to the back door. I opened it, picked Beth up from the seat, and hurried with her through the torrent to the shelter of the porch. Once we were under cover, I knocked on the door with my free hand. Beth opened her eyes slightly and looked at me. I didn't know in that moment if it was stranger for her or me standing there with her in my arms.

The door finally opened, and Allie peeked her head outside. "Oh, heavens!" she said when she saw us. "What on earth happened?"

"Beth's a little beat up right now," I answered. "Do you mind if we come in?"

"Of course not." She opened the door. "Come inside out of that mess."

I carried Beth into the house and laid her down on the couch in the living room. Edward was sitting in a rocking chair and staring at a television screen. Only there was no show on, just static. He focused on the black and white dots despite our arrival. Allie stepped out for a second and came back with a bowl of chicken noodle soup on a silver platter, the same one, in fact, that she served pie from when Linden and I first visited their home.

She laid the platter down on the coffee table and sat next to Beth on the couch. "Did you know that chicken noodle soup fixes everything?" she asked me and then dipped a spoon into the bowl.

"I did not," I replied.

"Oh, yes." She held the spoonful of broth an inch from Beth's mouth. "I bet if Hitler's mother served him chicken noodle soup more often, World War Two would've never happened."

"Is that so?" I played along, opting to not point out the illogic of her statement.

Just then, Teenage Beth came into the living room from a hallway leading to the back of the house. She was wearing a Pink Floyd t-shirt and, with her hair mussed up, appearing as if she had just gotten out of bed. She saw me and winked at me. Allie noticed her and frowned.

Meanwhile, Adult Beth wasn't accepting the chicken noodle soup. Her eyes were wide open, but it was as if she were in a trance.

"What's for dinner?" asked Teenage Beth, evidently oblivious to the presence of her older self.

Allie sighed. "Same thing we always have," she replied, placing the untouched spoon back in the bowl. "Ham hocks and pigs' feet."

"Jesus Christ!" exclaimed Teenage Beth. "Can't we ever eat anything normal?!"

"You watch your language, young lady!" said Allie. "Don't

you ever use the Lord's name in vain in this house!"

"Fine!" she said. "I'll leave then!" She went to the front door and opened it. It was still raining heavily outside. "On second thought, I'll go back to my room." She slammed the door and disappeared down the hall.

"You'll have to excuse her," Allie said to me. "She's going through one of those phases."

She placed her hand on Adult Beth's forehead and quickly pulled it away. "Oh, my."

"Is she hot?" I asked.

"She's freezing," she answered. "Pretty soon, she'll be dead."

"Well, that's concerning." I leaned forward and put my lips next to Beth's ear. "I'm not sure what's going on here, but I need you back with me. Remember, you're the one in control."

Little Beth came in through the back door, soaking wet and crying. "There's a man outside!" she screamed. "He tried to kill me."

"Don't be so dramatic," Allie told her. "And change out of those clothes before you catch a cold."

"I'm telling you the truth!" cried Little Beth.

I got up from the chair and went to her. "Show me," I told her.

She shook her head. "I'm not going back out there," she said, sobbing.

"Tell you what. I'll go look. How does that sound?"

She nodded and wiped away her tears. "Be careful."

I opened the door and stepped out on the porch. The wind was blowing so hard I could barely stand still. I looked out across the land behind the house. At first, I saw nothing, but then a man dressed in a tattered, black suit appeared in the cornfield. His eyes glowed red. His face was covered in soot, and his thick, dark hair was slicked back. The rain pounded him, but he did not move. I willed an opened umbrella into my hand and held it over my head. Despite my better judgment, I descended the porch steps toward him.

I walked across the grass as the water pelted the top of the umbrella. Evidently, I posed no threat to the strange man because he made no sudden movements as I got closer to him.

About halfway to where he was standing, I turned back toward the house. Little Beth was standing at the edge of the porch, shaking from the cold. I stopped about three feet from the man.

He stared straight at me, unflinchingly.

"Who are you?" I asked.

He grinned and showed rotten, yellowing teeth. "I am the harvester of souls," he said. "I've come for the girl."

"I'm sorry. You can't have her."

He laughed, and the earth shook below my feet. Before I could react, he brushed past me and sprinted toward the porch. Little Beth screamed. The man leapt up onto the porch and grabbed hold of her. I ran after them, but it was too late. Once he had her, they both disappeared into a cloud of black smoke. At a loss, I willed the umbrella to vanish and went back into the house.

I quickly made my way to the living room and was glad to see that Adult Beth hadn't moved from the couch, not so much so to discover that she was still paralyzed. "Okay," I told her close to her ear. "I *really* need you to come back to me now. Things are getting super freaky."

Edward, who hadn't budged from his chair in front of the television, turned his head and looked at me. "Ain't no use now," he said. "They all go away some time."

Just when things couldn't have gotten worse, Beth's body began to tremble. Her eyes still transfixed on nothing, she shook as if she were having a seizure. I tried to hold her down, but it was no use. Edward, of course, was no help at all. As Beth continued to vibrate, lights shot out of both of her pupils like laser beams and onto the ceiling. More spontaneous illumination escaped from various orifices, causing her to appear as if she were a human disco ball.

Allie was nowhere to be seen. I took a step back from Beth as a crack suddenly appeared in her forehead and slowly crept its way down her face to her stomach. I shielded my eyes as the brightness emanating from the opening became blinding. Through a small sliver between my fingers, I watched as the familiar crimson creature pushed its demon hands out of the crevice and pushed open Beth's body. The beast climbed out of Beth's lifeless shell and leapt onto the coffee table. As soon as it was freed, Beth's split carcass vanished, blinding light and all.

Allie entered the room with a blueberry cobbler on her signature silver platter. "What in the name of all that's—"

Before she could finish her sentence, the crimson creature lunged at her, knocking both her and the blueberry cobbler to the ground. The monster pounced on top of Allie and sliced her face with its sharp claws. Allie struggled and pleaded for help. I picked up a vase and smashed it over the beast's head. It didn't even phase it. I tried pushing it off Allie, but the monster only shoved me into the wall. It mauled Allie until she fought no more.

After the creature was finished with Allie, it turned its attention to me. Edward continued to watch pixilated snowflakes on the television. The monster dived at me, but I quickly jumped out of the way. It ran headfirst through a window in the living room, shattering glass into shards that fell onto the ground. The impact didn't stop the creature. It landed on its feet outside in the grass and then sprinted through the rain toward the highway. Then it merged into the darkness.

"What'd I tell ya?" Edward said without taking his eyes off the static. "They all go away some time."

Chapter Twenty-Seven

Every now and then, I question my life choices. There was the one time when I was in an inmate's dream and he tortured a man because he owed him drug money. There was another time when I pretended to be a serial killer's accomplice, so I could discover the grisly details of how he murdered his victims. And now, driving through an imaginary thunderstorm and chasing a demonic, red monster, I couldn't help but wonder if I might've been better suited to be a chef.

I finally caught up with the creature in the field where Beth had been discovered. It was running around in a circle near the same spot I found her lying unresponsive in the grass. I parked Beth's car by the side of the road. I opened the door and willed another umbrella to appear in my hand. I stepped outside and watched as the beast continued to chase its tail in the same three-hundred-sixty-degree pattern. Every few seconds, the creature let out a piercing shriek as if it had been wounded.

I slowly made my way toward the creature, careful not to alarm it as I approached. When I reached it, I noticed a familiar mist surrounding the area the monster was encircling. Suddenly, the beast ran straight into the haze. It bounced off what, not surprisingly, turned out to be another force field and landed with a thud on the ground. It got up and slammed into it again with the same result. After the monster hit the earth a second time, it started to shriek so loud I had to cover my ears. On the bright side, it wasn't trying to kill me.

I moved closer to the blockade and noticed that it extended vertically far into the sky. I reached my hand out toward it. The creature watched in awe as I barely touched it with my finger and was met with less resistance. It reacted the way a caveman might when seeing fire for the first time. Whatever lay on the other side obviously held some significance, so I took a step back and closed my eyes. I willed myself to transport into the center of the enclosure.

Once inside, there was an immediate change. It wasn't raining or thundering. In fact, the sun shone down exclusively on that particular spot. It was calm and peaceful, the exact opposite of the tempest outside. No longer needing the umbrella, I willed it to dematerialize. Through the fog, I saw the creature looking in at me. No wonder it wanted to cross the barrier. I held out my hand and beckoned it to join me. It shook its head and shrieked again.

I cautiously moved my hand toward the inside of the wall. Although it was just as fuzzy as the outside, it didn't push me away. I slowly put my fingers through the static barricade. They glowed as they penetrated the force field but came out safely on the other side. I extended the rest of my hand and held it out toward the creature. Half-expecting the monster to tear it off, I was pleased when the beast gently took my hand into its own.

"I'm going to bring you in," I told it, a metallic echo of my voice reverberating as it traversed the otherworldly obstruction.

The creature nodded. I coaxed it into the barrier, and, like my hand, it was able to cross over without incident. The only difference was that as each part of the monster's body passed the dividing line, it transformed into Beth's. Eventually, she was standing before me shivering, nude and soaking wet. I quickly conjured a blanket and covered her with it. Her lips quivered as she wrapped the comforter around her.

"That's the second time you've seen me naked, Max," she said, trembling. "Hardly seems fair. Does it?"

"I'm glad you're back to yourself again," I said, ignoring her comment.

"Me too," she said and shut her eyes. "It's a lot warmer on this side." She stopped shaking and the water on her evaporated. She opened her eyes and dropped the blanket to the ground. To my relief, she was wearing clothes she'd willed to materialize. "So, what now?"

"We go back to your parents' house and try again."

"No. I just want to get it over with. I remember leaving that night. It was no different than any other time."

"Okay. Do you remember what happened when you got here?"

"It's still blurry."

I motioned outside of the sanctuary she'd created. "Then we'll have to go out there and retrace your steps."

She shook her head. "I can't. I just got in here. It's terrible out there."

"You said you wanted to get it over with."

"I lied."

"Beth, it's the only way. Don't worry. I'll be with you the whole time."

She stalled, but then realized I wasn't backing down. "Can I at least have a minute?"

"Of course."

Beth stayed completely still for a moment as the rain pounded all around us, but not a single drop on our heads. She took a deep breath and exhaled. The force field dissipated as did the storm I thought would never end. The sun that radiated solely on us faded away too. Only the moon provided illumination in the darkness. Beth hesitantly looked at her car by the side of the road.

"I'm prolonging it," she said. "Aren't I?"

"That's not for me to say," I replied. "But if it's causing you pain, it may be time to face it."

She took my hand, and, together, we walked to the car. When we reached the driver's side, I tried to let go, but she held on tightly, gripping her fingers over mine. She looked at me pleadingly. In that moment, I felt worse for her than I ever had. Not caring how it might be construed, I leaned in and hugged her. She released my hand and hugged me back. I pulled away from her and motioned to the driver-side door.

"Were you in the car when your attacker arrived?"

She nodded. "I had run out of gas," she answered. "I was going to call Bobby, but my cell phone was dead."

I opened the car door. "Get in." After she reluctantly sat

down behind the wheel, I closed the door and went around to the passenger's side. I got in and shut the door. "So, then what happened?"

"I, uh, couldn't charge my phone, so I decided to walk to the nearest town." She looked into the rearview mirror. "But then, uh…I'm sorry. I can't do this."

"Yes, you can. What did you see in the mirror?"

She started breathing heavily. "Headlights."

"Show me."

The headlights appeared in the mirror, slowly approaching us. The beams were too bright for me to make out what kind of vehicle it was. The light flooded the inside of Beth's car so much, in fact, that I had to turn away from it for fear of being blinded. Beth hyperventilated. I put my hand on her back to try and calm her down. I considered aborting, but we were so close, and I didn't know if we'd ever get to that point again.

"Did the driver come to you or did you get out of the car?" I asked.

"I-I-can't remember," she said, her breaths getting shorter. "Please don't make me." She tried starting the engine, but it only sputtered. "I gotta get out of here!" She went to open the door, but it was locked. "Did you lock me in here?! Why would you do that?!"

"You know that I didn't."

She struggled with the lever, but it was jammed. "Look. I changed my mind. Okay? Now open the door!"

"Beth, stop it! If you keep running away from it, it's only going to catch up with you again. It has power over you. If you face it, you gain that power back."

She let go of the lever and sat still. She slowed her breathing down and gripped the steering wheel tightly. She looked into the rearview mirror directly at the headlights. They suddenly went dark. I turned around to see the vehicle. There was a haze around it, so it was still difficult to see. Beth opened the car door with no problem. She glared at me with a disdain in her eyes I hadn't seen before.

"You're a persistent son of a bitch," she said. "Aren't you?"

"I'm only trying to help you," I said.

"Well, come on then. Let's end this mystery together."

She got out of the car and closed the door. I climbed out of the passenger's side and came around behind her. In the mist, the other vehicle's door opened, and the sound of footsteps hit the pavement. A shadowy figure closed the door and walked toward us. As it approached, a scraping sound emanated from the concrete, growing louder as it got closer. When the figure finally emerged, standing before Beth as clear as day and holding a shovel in one hand, I froze.

"Daddy?" she said.

"Hey, little girl," Edward said vacantly then lifted the shovel and swung it hard across her face.

Chapter Twenty-Eight

Everything went completely dark. For a moment, I thought the shock of what happened caused so much distress that Beth's brain stopped functioning. Just as I feared that I was stuck in the sliver of a window between being connected and prematurely ejected back into reality, I spotted Beth in the distance. A warm glow surrounded her as she sat lotus style and floated aimlessly into the void.

I noticed that I emanated the same light. It extended only a foot beyond my body but was bright enough to help me get my bearings. I tried to move toward her, but, since there was no ground to walk on, I just spiraled off into another direction. When I finally stopped spinning, I pushed my arms out as if I were in water and thrust myself forward. I kicked my feet as well, repeating both actions until I was, quite literally, swimming after her.

Since I was moving faster than she was, I inevitably caught up with her. Her eyes were closed, but she seemed very much aware. She reminded me of one of those meditation gurus that emit energy despite remaining totally still. I came to a halt right by her side and waved my hand in front of her face. She didn't react. I tapped her on the shoulder even though I felt like I was intruding somehow.

"I know you're there, Max," she said without opening her eyes. "You don't have to get weird."

"Where are we?" I asked.

"The end of the line. This is where I get off."

"I don't understand."

"I'm never going to wake up. The least you can do is let me transition to the afterlife in peace."

"Beth, you can't just give up."

She opened her eyes. "No? My father tried to kill me, Max. Not only that. He murdered five women."

"We don't know that for sure."

"You might not, but I do. About twenty years ago, he left home and came back early the next morning. His clothes had red blotches on them. He told my mom and me that he hit a deer. I found a girl's blouse in his truck that afternoon, stained just the same. I wanted so badly to tell my mom but never did."

"Why not?"

"Because I was only twelve and he was my father. I ignored it."

"But it happened again?"

She nodded. "Two weeks later. Only this time it was a blood-stained shovel and another excuse that didn't add up. They started talking about two girls that went missing on the news. Both on the same nights my father came home unusually late and with evidence I chose to disregard. I went into full blown denial."

"And then?"

"They stopped talking about it, and eventually I blocked it out completely. But then, seven years later, during my first spring semester in college, another girl went missing. This one was from Ohio, so I didn't even give it a second thought. Besides, I had buried what I'd seen years earlier deep in my memory. It wasn't until 2008, when it happened again close to Louisville that I became obsessed."

"With the killer?"

She nodded. "And the victims."

She looked upward into the darkness, and, directly above us, a pattern of stars appeared.

They were still at first, twinkling as they would in the night sky. But then they started to swirl. I watched as they broke off into little clusters and danced around in a seemingly random fashion.

They became much more ordered, however, and, in their smaller groups, fused together to form numbers. As a whole, they created a familiar vertical sequence. "2-6-7-21-31."

"Mary Madsen was killed May 7, 1989," said Beth. "Linda Kassi died two weeks later."

The "7" and "21" broke away from the series of numbers and began a new, horizontal line above the original one. More stars came to life, gravitated toward each other, and shaped into new numbers that landed on either side of both the "7" and the "21." The first line read "5-7-89" and the second one read "5-21-89." The "2," "6," and "31" floated up from the vertical sequence and joined the horizontal one.

"Ashley Rogers didn't return home the night of March 2, 1996," Beth continued.

"Macie Lox and Rhonda Sinclair suffered similar fates on June 6, 2006, and August 31, 2008 respectively."

One last batch of stars emerged from the darkness, divided into sets, and completed the cosmic list of murder victim death days. As gratifying as it was to finally see the mystery unfold, I felt foolish for not solving it earlier when I read about the five women online. The article mentioned the dates, but I didn't even think to make the connection. It's amazing how something can be right under your nose yet somehow you overlook it.

"They were a lot like me," said Beth. "Young and still figuring out their lives. Then along came evil. Like a tornado, it scooped them up and blew them out into oblivion. I wanted the authorities to find the source of that evil so badly. I followed every new development no matter how minute. I needed to see the killer's face, so I could finally concretize it and rid myself of an uncertainty that had plagued me for years. But I guess it's like they say. Be careful what you wish for."

"I'm sorry, Beth," I told her, not knowing what else to say.

"He killed my dog too. I saw him do it with a kitchen knife. I tried so hard to convince myself that it didn't happen that I blamed myself. I even started to believe that I was the one that butchered that poor animal. I wanted him to be innocent so much that I was willing to carry the guilt. I'm not doing it anymore." She waved her hand and the stars vanished, leaving us in the darkness again. "Even if I could wake up, I don't know that I want to anymore."

"Now, wait a second. It doesn't have to be that bleak."

"My father's a serial killer, Max. It doesn't get much bleaker than that."

"Okay, but what about your mother? She's a victim as much as you are. If you give up, she'll have no one."

"Way to lay on the guilt, padre."

"I'm serious."

"She won't be around forever. And then what will I have?"

"Lots of things."

"Name one."

"You're a great artist."

"No, I'm not."

"Yes, you are. That painting in your apartment was amazing. Look, I can't even begin to imagine how you feel right now. But I do know that time heals, and, as much as this moment hurts, it will pass."

"What if it doesn't?"

"It will if you don't give up. There are bad things out there, and some of them are closer to home than we ever thought they'd be, but we have to keep going. Otherwise, the bad things take over and there's no one left to fight them."

"I appreciate what you're trying to do, Max, but I need to be alone right now."

"Are you sure that's for the best?"

"It's what I want."

"I don't know that I'm comfortable leaving you."

She looked at me with sadness in her eyes. "Please. It's not like I'm going anywhere."

I hesitated. "Okay, but I'll be back later."

"Goodbye, Max."

"I'll see you soon, Beth," I said, and then reluctantly withdrew from her mind.

Chapter Twenty-Nine

Once I was back in the hospital room, I waited a few minutes before leaving. I knew that technically she wanted to be alone, but I couldn't bring myself to go just yet. I got up from my chair and stood beside the bed. I reached out and took her hand, holding it gently. Although she couldn't respond, I hoped that she felt it inside, perhaps comforting her in the desolate place I had left her.

"The world's a better place with you in it, Beth," I said. "No matter how dark it may get, you're still a light."

A doctor came into the room. "Hello," he said.

"Hello," I reciprocated and then let go of Beth's hand. "I'll get out of your way."

"You're fine." He checked her vital signs and then started to leave. "Everything looks good."

"So, what would keep her from being able to wake up at this point?"

"Well, she's still very healthy. Most of the bruising has healed. Beyond that, it just depends on when she's ready. I've had some patients wake up weeks before we expected, and others stay unconscious for months. Everybody's different. Sometimes it comes down to will."

I nodded, failing to mention that fact that her will had been all but destroyed. "Thank you, Doctor."

We left the room together, and he went on to see another patient. I walked into the waiting room to tell Linden the news, but he was nowhere to be found. I looked through the open curtains of a window to see that it was dark outside. Like many times before, my work had caused me to lose track of time.

I pulled out my phone to see that it was eleven thirty p.m. I stepped out of the waiting room and approached the late-shift nurse at the receptionist's desk.

"Did you happen to see an FBI agent leave earlier?" I asked.

"Oh, sure," she said facetiously. "And then the secret service came through and had a parade." She handed me a note. "He left this for you."

Essentially, the paper said that Linden had gone back to the hotel and to call him first thing in the morning. I couldn't help but realize the irony. He spent countless hours in a hospital waiting room, watching soap operas and anticipating me identifying Beth's attacker, but, when I finally did, he was literally asleep on the job. I thanked the sarcastic nurse and headed for the exit.

Since Linden had ditched me, I took an Uber to the hotel. The driver proceeded to share the history of Louisville, going on and on about how much the city changed in the fifty years he'd lived there. It's not that I wasn't interested, but after finding out that Edward Martin was the Highway Killer, it was difficult to focus on anything else. When we reached the hotel, I thanked him for sharing and gave him an extra tip.

Once inside my room, I plopped down on the bed and closed my eyes. They suddenly opened again. As tired as my body was, my mind didn't want to cooperate. I turned on the television hoping that it would put me to sleep. No such luck. I turned it off and tried counting sheep, but, as each one leapt over the proverbial fence it, transformed into Edward midway. He'd land on the other side holding his shovel and grinning maliciously. Unable to take it any longer, I reached for my cell phone and called Jessica.

"Hello?" a drowsy voice answered.

"Katie?" I said, surprised to hear her. "What are you doing with your mom's phone?"

"I'm sleeping in your room tonight," she replied, sounding slightly more alert. "Mom didn't hear her phone ring over her snoring."

I laughed. "That sounds about right. What made you sleep in our room? You haven't done that in years."

"I don't know. Is that not okay?"

"Of course, it is."

"Why are you calling so late?"

"I think we may have solved the case."

"That's great. When will you be coming home?"

"Soon. I'll let you go. I know it's late and a school night."

"Okay. Hey, Dad. Guess what?"

"What?"

"I think I'm mastering the mind reading thing. Today in English, I was able to go the whole period without knowing what perverted thoughts Mr. Yuri was having about Brianna Sanders."

"That's good that you're getting control over it, but you might warn Brianna to not be alone with Mr. Yuri."

"I will."

"I'm proud of you, Katie. I'm lucky to be your dad."

"Well, don't get all mushy about it."

I chuckled. "Fair enough. I'll let you get back to sleep. Tell Mom I'll call her tomorrow."

"'Kay. Love you, Dad."

"Love you too, peanut. Sweet dreams."

After I got off the phone with Katie, I went right to sleep. Never underestimate the power of hearing the voice of a loved one. Mind you, the effect only lasted the night. The next morning, I awoke to the abrasive and unnerving sound of pounding on my door. I put on my bath robe and looked through the peephole. Through the fisheye lens, I saw Linden in the hallway, already dressed in one of his three, token FBI suits.

"Come on, Crawford," he said into the door. "Let me in."

I reluctantly opened the door. "Always a pleasure, Agent Linden."

"It's about time." He let himself in. "Well? What did you find out?"

I sat on the edge of the bed and pointed to the desk chair near the T.V. "You might want to sit down."

"Son of a bitch." He sat down in the chair. "You solved it. Didn't you?"

I nodded. "It was Edward. He attacked Beth and, apparently, killed the others."

"Are you shittin' me?"

"You know I wouldn't shit you, Linden."

"This is incredible." He leapt up from his chair. "Well, come on. Why aren't you dressed yet? We gotta get back to the hospital. I need to contact Sheriff Luttrell and get an officer down there to guard him. Seriously, why aren't you dressed yet?"

After negotiating five minutes to brush my teeth and throw on some clothes, I met Linden outside the hotel, and we drove to the hospital. Upon arrival, he immediately made his way to the wing where Edward had been admitted as a patient. I, on the other hand, went to see Beth. I felt like I'd given her ample time to float in space contemplating her existence and was ready to go back in to support her in any way that I could.

When I reached her room, I saw that the door was open. I stepped inside and came to an abrupt halt. The bed was empty. In fact, a nurse was stripping the sheets, evidently preparing the room for the next patient. My heart sank. I moved back into the hallway and, right as I was about to inquire at the receptionist's desk, heard footsteps behind me. I turned to see Beth sitting in a wheelchair with a portable IV, a nurse standing behind her.

She smiled weakly. "Hello, Max," she said.

Chapter Thirty

Beth woke up from her coma at three a.m. As soon as the nurses realized she had become conscious, they began a routine that they'd been trained on and, thankfully, were able to complete successfully. First, Beth was asked a sequence of questions including having her tell them her name, her age, and the president of the United States. I wondered if some patients requested to be put back to sleep after recalling the latter.

Next, they moved on to a series of simple physical exercises with her such as trying to get her to wiggle her toes, stretch her arms out, and eventually sit up in bed. Not only did Beth pass all tests with flying colors, but she impressed the hospital staff with how quickly she was able to do so. Finally, and this is where I showed up, she was helped out of bed into a wheelchair and taken out of her room to reorient her to her surroundings.

"Hello, yourself," I said. "How are you feeling?"

"Like I've been run over by a bulldozer," she replied.

"Let's get you back into your room," the attending nurse told her.

I stepped aside as the nurse rolled Beth into the hospital room. I walked in after them and stood close to the bed. I couldn't believe it. I'd heard of people making miraculous recoveries but had, up until now, never witnessed it firsthand. Once they reached the bed, the nurse helped Beth out of the wheelchair. She held the back of Beth's gown together in an effort to maintain modesty and then pulled open the sheets of the freshly made bed.

"Don't worry about trying to cover me," Beth said, probably saying too much too soon.

"He's already seen my ass twice. One more time won't make any difference."

Once Beth was lying down, the nurse, whose face was now turning red, tucked in her patient and checked her vital signs. After a few minutes, the nurse left with the wheelchair, leaving me alone with Beth for the first time in reality. There was a moment of awkward silence.

Or maybe I was making it awkward in my head, and Beth had simply worn herself out making blatant comments about the number of times I'd seen her naked.

"Can I get you anything?" I finally broke the quiet.

She sluggishly shook her head. "They called my mom," she said, closing her eyes.

"She's on her way."

"Don't talk unless you have to. I'll be right here till she arrives."

We sat there together for about an hour. When Allie got there, she was so elated to see that her daughter had come back to her that she broke into tears. I left the room, so they could have some time alone together. I crossed over to the wing where Edward was and found that the local police were already on the scene. Linden was talking to an officer stationed outside Edward's room. He saw that I'd arrived and quickly came over to me.

"Did you see Beth?" he asked.

"Yes," I told him. "She's awake."

"Holy shit. How long?"

"Since three a.m. this morning." I motioned to Edward's room. "What's next for him?"

"We're still working on that. He'll probably be transferred to a facility in a day or two."

"Will he even be able to stand trial?"

He shrugged. "Either way, he's not going anywhere for a long time."

I nodded. "Can I see him? I'd like to try to read his mind and see if I can get some evidence."

"Be my guest."

I walked past Linden, gave a nod to the officer, and entered

Edward's room. He was sitting in a chair, wearing a hospital gown and staring out the window. He rocked back and forth in what appeared to be a self-soothing motion, mumbling to himself. I stood right beside him, but he didn't seem to know I was there. I blocked his view of the outside world and stared him straight in the face.

For the first time, my own thoughts reflected back at me. It was as if his brain had become so broken nothing could get inside. I found it unsettling and quickly turned away. He finally realized I was standing in his way and slowly lifted his head to look at me. His eyes seemed lost in their sockets, like fish that had been forced onto land and were aimlessly fighting to find their way back to water.

"The bible's missin' some pages," he said listlessly.

Choosing not to respond, I left the room to join Linden in the hallway. "There's nothing there," I told him.

"I could've told you that, Crawford," said Linden. "The guy's cuckoo for Cocoa Puffs."

"So, what now?"

He smiled, genuinely to my astonishment. "We'll take over from here. You've done some great work, Max. Go be with your family."

Then again, I wasn't too surprised. Once Linden got what he needed, he became much more relaxed. "Okay. I suppose I'll just book a flight then."

"It's already been done. You fly out at eleven a.m. I'll have a car take you to the hotel to gather your things and then on to the airport. You can expect compensation in the next few days."

"I'm not worried about that. If it's alright with you, I'd like to say goodbye to Beth."

"Of course," he said, extending his hand. "Good luck to you, Crawford."

I accepted cautiously, expecting there to be a catch. There wasn't. "So long, Agent Linden."

I walked out of the ward and made my way back to Beth's room. It felt strange to me having spent so much time on the case and now it was over. Not that I wasn't thrilled to be going home. I suppose I just never got used to things ending as abruptly as they do sometimes. I stopped outside Beth's room and saw Allie by her side. The two seemed to be in a serious conversation so I waited. Beth saw me through the window and grinned. Allie turned, noticed I was there, and quickly came out to see me. She hugged me immediately.

"Thank you so much," she said. "I don't know what you did, but I'm forever in your debt."

"It wasn't me. It was her. Your daughter's a strong woman."

She let go of me. "Will you be staying a while?"

"Actually, I'll be heading home in a few hours." I motioned toward Beth. "Do you mind if I have a minute with her before I go?"

"Of course not. You take your time."

I went in and sat in the familiar chair beside her, relieved that I could talk to her face to face and not have to intrude on her thoughts. "When I left you, you were in a pretty dark place. What happened?"

"I was floating there, thinking about everything, when I felt something push me. At first, I thought I was having some sort of physical reaction and that it would pass. But it kept propelling me forward, getting stronger and stronger like heavy wind gaining momentum. I tried resisting, but it was futile." She paused for a moment, seemingly worn out from talking. "And then…"

"It's okay if you need to rest."

She slowly shook her head. "I've been resting long enough. After it forced me along for a while, the sun appeared in the distance. It sped up exponentially and then hurled me directly into the massive fireball. That's when I woke up."

"Wow. I guess sometimes will transcends the mind."

"Will had nothing to do with it. I wasn't ready to come back yet."

"Maybe you were and just didn't realize it. Regardless, you're here now. The question is what are you going to do?"

She closed her eyes and laid her head against the pillow. "The families…I'm going to contact them."

"What families?"

"Of the others. Whoever's still living, I'm going to do whatever I can to help ease their pain."

"That's noble of you, but what about you? What are you going to do to take care of yourself?"

"I'll stay with my mom for a while. Go back to work."

"At the gallery?"

"Hell, no." She opened her eyes and looked at me. "Somebody told me I was pretty good at painting. Thought I'd give it another go."

"That's great, Beth. I'm proud of you."

She smiled faintly but it quickly faded. "My mom doesn't know yet."

"She will as soon as she goes to see him. There's an officer outside his room."

"If it's alright, I want to be the one to tell her. I'd rather her not find out that way."

"Of course."

"Did you see him?"

"Yes."

"And?"

"He's getting worse. You know, I was thinking. It is very possible that he didn't recognize you when he attacked you."

"I know he didn't. That doesn't make it any better. The fact he had it in him toward anyone makes him a monster. I don't think I'll ever be able to look at him again."

"That's understandable. I'll be leaving in a few hours. I just wanted to see you before I left."

"I'm sure your family will be glad to see you. They're lucky to have you."

"You sure you'll be okay?"

"The way I see it I have two choices. Either wallow in the misery of the past or try to make a better future. The first one sounds like a pretty awful way to live, so I'll go with the second."

"Sounds like a good decision." I suddenly felt awkward. "Well, I, uh—"

"Don't make it weird, Max. But, then again, the whole thing has been weird. Hasn't it?"

"Definitely." I stood. "Goodbye, Beth. Take care of yourself."

"Goodbye, Max." She held out her hand. "Thank you."

I took her hand and felt a slight squeeze. "You're welcome."

I left her room shortly thereafter and told Allie to call me if they needed anything. I then followed Linden's instructions and was taken back to the hotel to collect my things. The driver was the same one that picked me up at the airport, and, like before, didn't say one word to me the entire time. That was okay with me. My thoughts kept me company from the time we departed the hospital to the moment I got on the plane.

When I initially took the case, I had selfish intentions. I wanted to learn more about the mind in between life and death but, in the process, discovered that the human will was much more intriguing. Beth was not only overcoming the physical aspects of her circumstances but also determined to take control of the psychological and emotional ones as well. Every time I entered her subconscious, my goal was to help her, yet, in the end, she inspired me.

As I sat on the plane waiting to take off, my phone buzzed. It was Jessica. "Hello?" I answered.

"Hey," she said. "Sorry, I missed your call last night. I was out."

"So, I heard. We solved the case."

"Really?! So, who attacked her?"

I hesitated. "Her father."

She was silent for a moment. "That's horrible."

"Yeah, but, the good news is she's awake. I think you'd like her. She's got quite a spirit."

"I'm glad you were there for her. Where are you now?"

"On a plane coming back to you."

"That's wonderful! We've really missed you, Max."

"I've missed you too."

The announcement to turn off all electronical devices came over the PA system. After exchanging "I Love You's," I got off the phone with Jessica and looked out the window of the plane. As we started our ascent, I thought about the challenges Beth had ahead of her and had no doubt she would face them. I thought about Jessica and how fortunate I was to have her in my life. I thought about Katie and how I'd be there when she needed me. I felt optimistic about the future. After all, in a few short hours, I would be home.

About the Author

Matthew Franks lives in Arlington, Texas, with his beautiful wife and children. He studied psychology and creative writing at Louisiana State University then obtained a Master's Degree in counseling from Texas State University. When he's not working on his next story, he's counseling adolescents or trying to keep up with his three highly energetic daughters.

Bibliography
The Monster Underneath
The Orion Medallion
When Beth Wakes Up

Curious about other Crossroad Press books?
Stop by our site:
http://store.crossroadpress.com
We offer quality writing
in digital, audio, and print formats.

Milton Keynes UK
Ingram Content Group UK Ltd.
UKHW040700031224
3343UKWH00040B/635

9 781950 565382